DEAD OF WINTER

A Novel by

Gil Burgess

First published by AuthorHouse 04/07/04

ISBN: 1-4184-1488-3 (e-book)
ISBN: 1-4184-0778-X (Paperback)

Library of Congress Control Number: 2003096881

Printed in the United States of America
Bloomington, Indiana

This book is printed on acid free paper.

LAMBDA LODGE AND RESORT

CABIN 1

CABIN 2

CABIN 3

PARKING

RAINBOW HOUSE

MAIN LODGE

TENNIS COURTS

PARKING

POOL

MT. NEBO HOUSE

MT. NEBO RD.

PARKING

DISCO

To RT. 210

DEDICATION

For my Father

If tears could build a stairway
And memories a lane,
I'd walk right up to heaven
And bring you home again.

PART I

THE GATHERING

Gil Burgess

Chapter 1 — NOVEMBER 23rd

The first snow came early, before Thanksgiving. Jonathan Myers looked out of the picture window of the lodge, watching the glistening flakes swirl and glide to earth. The ground sparkled and the trees bowed. He smiled. The first snowfall was special for him. It brought back many fond childhood memories of ice skating in the park and sledding down the many hills here in the Poconos, where he grew up. More than anything, however, he liked the stillness that accompanied the snow. The whole world became a more peaceful place.

He pushed himself away from the window, got his coat and stepped onto the porch that surrounded two sides of the lodge. He stood there, watching his breath in the cold, late afternoon air. He started toward the stairs, but stopped. He didn't want to trespass on Mother Nature's new, white blanket. Instead, he sat on one of the Adirondack chairs on the porch. In this quiet world he was in there were no people, no business to run, no problems to deal with, just contentment and peace of mind.

The sky was still heavy with snow, predictions were for 6 to 8 inches by morning. As he scanned the endless white vista he felt it a shame that plows would soon pass through, slicing it, cutting civilizations mark into nature's work. He sighed and looked up, the streetlights had come on. Even up here on a mountaintop in the Poconos, the glare of reality pierced through. The lights illuminated pools of diamonds beneath them, and even their harsh glare was softened.

As much as he loved summer, with its warm sun and color, Jonathan relished winter for its solitude. Even the lodge and the various buildings that comprised Lambda Lodge and Resort appeared more relaxed and tranquil. The whole mountain hibernated, warm and cozy under its soft white quilt.

He got up and walked to the far side of the porch, where the road, path would be a better term, wound its way up the crest of Mt. Nebo. Barely visible, on the far side of Mt. Nebo Road, sat the 3 small cabins that were part of the lodge complex. Secluded from view by a stand of large conifers, they were closed for the winter, since they were unheated. The only evidence of their existence was the small flight of stone steps that wound its way up from the road, then vanished into the forest floor. Now even that hint of their being there was obliterated by the storm. The grounds crew wouldn't even bother shoveling them, or the path, since no one would be using the cabins until late spring.

Even in the fading light of evening, however, these dark, cold cabins glowed warmly to Jonathan, maybe due to their deep color, the wood used in their construction many decades ago weathering and softening with age. He was truly happy here. Buying this place was the best thing he and Charlie could have done.

Leaving Manhattan and its mountains of skyscrapers was not a difficult decision for him, Charlie, however, had many misgivings. Having been born and raised in New York City he was leary of living so far from everything, not to mention running a resort.

When the lodge came up for sale about two years ago, Jonathan had immediately wanted to buy it. He saw the resort as a chance to escape the city and all its stresses, as well as a place where he and Charlie could retire and grow old together.

After almost 8 months of discussions and arguments, Charlie's fears were finally allayed. He did love the place, ever since their first visit. They'd been back several times over the past few years during summer, autumn as well as for New Year's Eves and found it a wonderfully relaxing place to be.

The rooms in Lambda Lodge, the main building, were small, but comfortable and cozy, consisting of a double bed, dresser, and a small sink. Rainbow House, one of the two other buildings on the property, had large rooms and private baths, and was relatively close to the lodge. Mt. Nebo House was built more like modern motel than a mountain lodge. The rooms were large with two queen size beds, private bathrooms and television sets, but it was the farthest down the mountain from the lodge and a treacherous walk during the winter. Despite its lack of amenities, Lambda Lodge was usually booked first, people like staying right in the center of the complex.

The staff at the lodge was consistent, the same waiters, bartenders and registration desk clerks were there year after year. This made guests feel like they were coming to visit family. The food was superb, the dining room had won several local awards for its cuisine and these were proudly displayed in the lobby.

When Jonathan finally broke down Charlie's defenses and he agreed to make an offer on the lodge, he thought it would be a matter of weeks, maybe a month or two before they could escape Manhattan for good. That was not to be. First the property had to be appraised, and all the buildings inspected. An accountant was hired to check the books to be sure the lodge was a good investment, for both Charlie and Jonathan and the bank. The final step was the negotiating of the price. After months of reports, inspections, offers and counter offers, the final price was agreed upon and the deal was finalized, and the papers signed.

Jonathan wanted to move right away, but Charlie, always pragmatic, reminded him that they couldn't simply walk away from their jobs. Both men had successful careers in Manhattan, Jonathan in an advertising firm on Madison Avenue, Charlie as an investment banker in The Bank of New York. They agreed to spend weekends at the lodge while they tied up all the loose ends at home, including the sale of their condo on the Upper East Side, then make the move. Finally, almost a year and a half later, they packed up their furniture and other possessions and left Manhattan for good.

"Here you are! I've been looking for you everywhere." Charlie came up behind him and wrapped his arms tightly around Jonathan's waist. Kissing his neck, he asked, "What's going on in that overactive brain of yours?"

Settling his head back on Charlie's shoulder, he sighed, "Nothing. Just watching the snowfall. Beautiful, isn't it? I could watch it forever."

"If you don't come in soon, you'll freeze here and get your wish! Come on in, dinner is almost ready."

They walked back into the lobby, the warm air taking Jonathan deeper into his relaxed frame of mind. This being a weeknight, and a snowy one, there were few guests in the dining room. Jonathan and Charlie stopped at each table, making sure everything was satisfactory, it was. They then sat at their usual table, just outside the swinging kitchen door, and Helen brought them their dinners. Contrary to the meals served to guests, their dinner was simple, grilled chicken, baked potato and salad. Dining as the guests did on a regular basis would add pounds quicker than any amount of exercise could keep in check.

Charlie began eating, Jonathan, however, was still in that other place. Smiling slightly, he watched Charlie for a moment, then picked up his knife and fork. "I'm glad we're here. Thank you."

Charlie stopped in mid-bite, "I should be thanking you. If you hadn't kept up your barrage we'd still be back in the city, stressed out and getting old before our time."

Jonathan agreed and they both started eating, their conversation centering on the upcoming New Year's Eve celebration they were planning. Both men were totally unaware of the approaching menace.

Chapter 2 — NOVEMBER 30th

Police in Dayton, Ohio, found few clues and only one possible suspect in the murder of Walter Marqueth, a wealthy business man and prominent member of the city's gay community. Patrol units responded to the scene after receiving calls from both Marqueth's neighbors and sister stating that he hadn't been seen in several days, and that his phone has been constantly busy, apparently off the hook.

Judith Wilset, Marqueth's sister, arranged to meet the officers at the house and let them in. Upon entering, they found the house dark, cold and eerily silent. Nothing on the first floor of the Tudor style home was disturbed and the officers asked Mrs. Wilset to remain downstairs while they searched the bedrooms upstairs. Several long minutes later, one of the officers returned and rushed out of the house, past the confused and now frightened woman. Minutes later more police units arrived, the area was cordoned off and a full-scale investigation was begun.

Detective Sam Ogsten interviewed Marqueth's neighbors while an uniformed policewoman saw to Mrs. Wilset. The neighbors could tell Detective Ogsten little. The last time they saw Marqueth was on Thanksgiving night when he returned from his sister's. "He wanted to spend some time with his boyfriend." Mr. Nash told them, "They arrived together. I guess Walter picked him up at his place."

"Did you hear or see anything out of the ordinary that night?"

Nash chuckled, "The whole thing is out of the ordinary. I mean, I don't care that Walt was gay, but he got hooked up with that young kid. Had to be at least a 15 to 20 year age difference between them. Well, to each his own I guess." Nash held his hands up defensively. "I can't tell you more than that. Only thing I know is that I went over there after Mrs. Wilset called me and said his line was constantly busy. When no one answered the door, or my calling out, I phoned her back and told her so."

"And when was that, sir?"

Nash put his hand on his chin, "I believe that would be last night, Monday. Yeah, it was Monday. I remember because my grandson was here and we were watching wrestling on TV. He loves that stuff."

Ogsten thanked Mr. Nash and returned to the house, now swarming with members of Dayton's crime scene division as well as the coroner.

"What can you tell me so far, Ted?" Ogsten asked Dr. Gaven.

13

"Not too much yet. Only things I am sure of so far are that he was strangled, and he's been dead for about 48 hours. Other that that..." his voice trailed off, and he shook his head. "We'll have the lab run a complete serology to determine if there were any drugs involved."

"What about prints?"

Gaven shook his head, "Not on the body. The house was too cold, and from the look of the bedroom, he'd just taken a shower. Besides, too much time has passed. Your best hope for prints would be from somewhere else in the house."

"I hope they find some." Ogsten sighed. "Okay, Ted. Thanks," he looked at the house, "I guess I'd better get in there and talk to his sister."

Mrs. Wilset was in the kitchen, at the back of the house, with Officer Jonson. Detective Ogsten could tell from the way her hand trembled when she picked up the cup in front of her that she was still very shaken. Jonson looked up at the detective and shook her head. Knowing what that meant, Ogsten nodded and headed back out to the entry foyer. The guys from the crime scene division were wrapping up their work, the body already on its way to the morgue. Ogsten stopped one of the men, "Anything?"

"Not much, Detective. We've got some prints, but they could turn out to be the victims. The only hair we found was gray, so it couldn't be of his young boyfriend, and there wasn't any blood at all. Pretty clean scene, if you ask me."

"Great. All right, thanks guys. Get on the prints right away. This guy could still be around."

"Detective!" It was Officer Jonson, "Mrs. Wilset wants to talk to you."

Ogsten rushed into the kitchen. Mrs. Wilset was still sitting at the table, her hands wrapped around the cup in front of her. She looked up at him through red, swollen eyes and managed a weak smile. "Detective, please sit down." she said as she patted the seat of the chair next to her.

"Mrs. Wilset," he said as he pulled out the chair and sat facing her, "I'm so sorry."

"Thank you, Detective." She took a deep breath, "I understand you need to ask me a few questions. What are they?"

"Well, I need you to describe your brother's boyfriend for us. How tall he is, color hair, eyes, any distinguishing characteristics he might have. Anything that could help us find him and bring him in for questioning."

"All right." Judith Wilset gave Ogsten as complete a description of her brother's boyfriend as she could. She had only seen him a few times over the time Marqueth and he had been dating.

Ogsten asked her if she could remember where he was from, what he did for a living. She couldn't.

"Mrs. Wilset, do you know anyone who might be able to give us this information?"

"I'm afraid not. Walter kept his personal life just that way. No one in the immediate family knew much about who his friends were." She was quiet for a while. "I'm ashamed. He was my brother, my only brother, and I never really knew all there was to him. Funny isn't it?"

Ogsten could only nod in agreement.

"Is there anything else, Detective? I really must be on my way. It's a long drive home."

"No. Thank you Mrs. Wilset. If there is anything you think of that might help, please don't hesitate to call me at the station." He handed her one of his cards. As she looked at the black print on the white background, tears filled her eyes. She pulled herself up, "I will, Detective. I will."

Detective Ogsten watched as she slowly walked through the house to the front door. She knew this was the last time she would ever be in this house, and she wanted to take in as much of it as she could. He couldn't help feel her pain.

"Was she able to give you much information?" Officer Jonson asked as she and Ogsten stood in the kitchen doorway.

"Not much. We'll have to interview his business associates and hope they can give us some leads. Maybe one of them will know who his boyfriend is."

"Chief? You busy?" Ogsten asked as he nudged open the door to Chief Myers' office.

Looking up from his cluttered desk, Chief Myers waved him in. "Well?" he asked.

"Not much, I'm afraid. We got some prints from the scene as well as a fairly good description of the boyfriend. That's about it. Hopefully the guys in the crime lab will come up with something. We should have the results in a day or two."

"Was there anything missing?"

Ogsten shook his head, "We can't tell, nor can his sister."

"Was there any cash, or credit cards in the house?"

"Yeah, in his wallet on the dresser we found some cash and one credit card, but he may have had more. We don't know."

"Do you think the boyfriend killed him?"

"It looks that way, but I can't say for sure."

Chief Myers got up and began pacing his small office. He thought better when he was moving. "Get a recent photo of Marqueth. Have it circulated to all the gay bars in the city. Somebody will know him, and they may know the boyfriend. Get in touch with the sister again. Have her come in to help the sketch artist in coming up with a composite. What was the name she gave you?"

Ogsten flipped the pages of notes he'd taken. "Ah, here it is. Zimens, John Zimens."

"Think it's real?"

"I don't know. Probably not. We can run it through N.C.I.C. while we wait for the lab results to come back."

"Let's hope that can tell us something."

Ogsten left the Chief to start work.

Chief Myers sat down and rubbed his face. He was tired, tired and a bit frightened. He looked at the photo he'd kept on his desk for the past 25 years, his ex-wife, and their only child, Jonathan. His eyes wandered to the phone. "No," he thought, "Not yet. I'm not ready to call him."

Chapter 3 — DECEMBER 2nd

Antone' Rios stepped off the Greyhound bus onto 11th Avenue, in Pittsburgh. From all he'd heard, he'd expected to find the city drab, dreary and dirty, but it was none of those things. As a matter of fact, it was quite an attractive city, from what he could see as he started walking aimlessly down Penn Avenue. At this early hour there were few people on the streets and traffic was light. He couldn't find a cab anywhere and continued walking, pulling his coat tighter around himself, the cold, damp morning air chilling him through to the bone. Having grown up and lived near Pheonix until he was 30, he was not accustomed to such dreadful weather. Sure it got cold in Arizona, but the air was never this oppressive.

"How can people live here?" he thought as he looked at the buildings, their windows reflecting back the heavy gray sky. He started looking for a place to get out of the weather and think. He was beginning to doubt his decision to stop here, but he had to get out of Ohio, the reality of what he'd done took over and he was terrified by it. "This has to stop," he told himself as he passed still dark storefronts, "Not all such men are bad. Not all of them want to hurt me." He was scared, by both what he'd done and by the fear of it happening again, but he wanted someone, needed the security and love.

Finally, after walking in the drizzle for about 30 minutes, he saw a coffee shop, DeLucas, straight ahead. He was hungry, and had to get out of this weather to think and plan. The warm air of the diner, permeated with the smell of frying bacon and fresh brewed coffee, engulfed him. At first he moved to the counter, but opted for a booth in the far corner instead, not wanting to attract any unwanted attention.

He picked up a menu from its chrome holder, more to keep from being seen than to decide what to order. He knew he must look awful. The bus ride had been longer than anyone could have expected due to bad weather in Ohio. He'd cleaned up the best he could in the men's room in the depot, but there was little he could do to hide the dark circles under his eyes, or the scruffy beard. Not wanting to carry them, he'd stored his canvass bags in a depot locker, taking only cash. Those bags contained all he owned, or had stolen, some clothes, a few pieces of jewelry he could pawn, and a bit more cash.

Without asking, the elderly waitress brought him coffee. "You look like you need this."

"It shows?" he croaked, his throat raw and sore.

She nodded. "What can I get you?"

Immediately engaging his charm, Antone' smiled, "How about a shower, a razor, and a soft bed?"

She laughed heartily. "I don't think that's on the menu, sweetheart, but I'll see what I can do. Now," she resumed her waitress position, "Let's try again. What can I get you?"

He ordered the house special, a hearty breakfast of eggs, any style, buckwheat pancakes, and homemade sausage, with more coffee.

"Good choice. That'll get you feelin' better."

"Yeah, I hope so," he agreed.

When the waitress, Millie, her name tag read, brought his breakfast, he asked if there was a local newspaper he could see.

"Sure, honey, I'll get it. You eat," she replied, pointing to the steaming plate in front of him.

He glanced through the paper, skimming it to see if there was anything about Marqueth's body being found, nothing. "Maybe they don't know," he hoped. He next turned to the section he needed to see, the personal ads. Nowadays, all newspapers printed ads for gays as well as straights seeking

23

'mates'. Most were just looking to get laid, fine by him. Scanning quickly, he found the section he needed. 'Men Seeking Men'. There were quite a few. He quickly eliminated the ads from men his own age or younger, and honed in on the ones from men over 50, there were 7 of them. Using a napkin, he copied the ad numbers as well as the paper's 900 number used for responses. He eliminated one from a married man who was looking for 'discrete man to man interludes'. "That's sick," he thought. Finishing as much of the huge meal as he could, he paid the check, leaving a sizable tip for Millie, and started to leave.

Millie stopped him at the door, "If you need a place to stay, maybe I can help. Friends of mine might have a room available. They rented it to a college kid this fall, but I think he had to drop out, wasn't doin' very well and his folks refused to keep payin' the tuition. It might be rented already, but it's worth a try. Their name's McNaulty, the house is on Spring Street, two blocks down and a block over, third house in on the right, number 37. Tell them

Millie sent you, my word is as good as gold with them."

Antone' was truly touched. He hadn't expected such small town kindness in a city. He wrote down the name and street on the napkin with the phone numbers he'd copied from the paper. "Thank you, Millie. I'll do that." He smiled and headed down the cold, bleak street.

Antone' found McNaulty's easily, and after mentioning Millie's name, they readily rented him the room. "Well, if Millie sent you." Mrs. McNaulty said as she handed him a pen to register, a smile wrinkling her face into a living prune. Antone' returned the smile and filled out the card. Putting her reading glasses on the end of her bird-like nose, Mrs. McNaulty examined it. "Ah, Mr. Zimza, is it? That's an unusual name."

"I know. It was altered when my grandfather came through Ellis Island," he lied. "The real family name is lost forever, I'm afraid."

"Oh, what a shame. A family must know its roots," she said as she filed the card in the desk draw in the living room. Raising the index finger of her right hand, emphasizing her point, she continued. "It's important, gives one a sense of history. How long will you be staying with us?"

"Probably only a few weeks. I'm on my way to New York, going to try my luck at modeling. Who knows, maybe I'll be on that billboard in Times Square wearing Calvin Kline underwear."

Mrs. McNaulty stopped on the worn staircase and turned to him, her face stern. "Oh my! I hope not. I don't approve of such things. You are quite handsome, but I'd prefer it if you kept your clothes on."

"Thank you." Antone' blushed a bit.

A cool smile passed across her lips as she turned and continued up the stairs. "Follow me. I'll show you to your room. It's towards the back of the hall, more private that way, and it's near the bathroom." She filled him in on the rules of the house on the way up. No drinking, no women, no loud noises after 10:00 P.M. A modest breakfast is provided daily, and the kitchen is available to use for cooking dinner, provided it is kept clean. Antone' listened half-heartedly, knowing he wouldn't be there that long.

The room was small, but comfortable. A single iron frame bed, a dresser, small sink as well as a rocking chair and floor lamp. The room smelled slightly of lemon scent Lysol and was a bit stuffy. Mrs. McNaulty opened the shade and window to let in the limited light and air out the musty smell. That done, she turned to Antone'. "There, what do you think? Not a palace, but clean and comfortable. I'll leave you to get settled in." As she finished the last statement, a puzzled look crossed her face. "Where are your bags?"

"Oh. I didn't want to lug them around. I stored them in a locker at the bus depot. Now that I have a place to call home, I'll get them and settle in."

"That was sweet of you to call this home. I'm glad you feel that way. Here's your key, and if you need anything we're right down stairs. Just knock on the door behind the desk, either my husband or myself are usually here." She left him then.

Antone' looked around the room, his forced smile fading fast. "I'd better hook up fast. This place will drive me batty!" He closed and locked the door behind him, leaving the window open. Heading toward the bus depot, he passed DeLucas, spotting Millie behind the counter he popped in. She smiled when she saw him approaching, "Well?" she asked.

He picked up her hands and kissed the back of them. "You're a doll. Thank you so much."

"Oh go on with you," Millie giggled. "I was glad to help. Don't let the McNaulty's scare ya none. They act tough, but they're sweet as sugar once you get to know them."

"I'm sure they are. I've got to get my things and settle in. I think we'll be seeing a lot of each other, I'll probably be eating here a lot."

"Oh good."

Squeezing her thick hands once more, Antone' said good-bye. Once outside, he turned and waved.

"Such a nice young man," Millie thought as she returned to her work.

Antone' retrieved his bags from the locker, and proceeded to the bank of pay phones across the hall. He punched in the code from the stolen AT&T calling card he'd taken from Walter Marqueth and waited, hoping it was still valid, it was. He went down the list of men he'd written down earlier in the day, leaving his name and McNaulty's phone number, saying he was interested in meeting. Much to his surprise, one of the men had called by the time he returned to McNaulty's. Mrs. McNaulty handed him the message, "May I use the phone? It's a local call."

"Of course. It's right there," she said, pointing to the small table in the living room.

When the phone was answered, he introduced himself.

"Oh yes," Richard said, his tone cheerful, "I'm glad you called back so soon."

"Well," he laughed, "It's nice to know someone would answer their messages so soon. You're Richard?"

"Yes."

"I'd like to know if we could meet sometime soon."

"That depends. Tell me about yourself."

Antone' described himself, his interests, hobbies, and goals in life. When he mentioned his age, Richard had a few misgivings, and several questions.

"You realize I'm in my 50's, don't you?"

"Yes."

"Why didn't you answer ads from men your own age? Surely you'd have more in common with them."

"No," Antone' answered quickly, "I wouldn't. Most men in their mid to late 30's are still growing up. I've always found myself getting bored with them. They lack depth and maturity. I was with my last lover for almost 6 years. We'd still be together if..." he began sobbing, "If he hadn't been taken from me so suddenly."

"Oh, I'm sorry. I didn't mean to upset you." Richard felt sympathy for this young stranger.

"No, that's all right. I'm okay." Antone' went on to tell Richard how he and Stan had met, fallen in love and been very happy together, despite their age difference. "We complimented each other beautifully," Antone' continued lying to Richard, "Stan was semi-retired, working 3 or 4 mornings a week. I'd call him during my lunch break every day. One day he didn't answer. At first I thought nothing of it, he'd probably gone shopping or to visit his sister, or out to lunch with friends. I tried him again at about 3:00, still no answer. That's when I started to get concerned. I got home at about 4:30 and called for him, but didn't get a response. Then I saw him," Antone's voice got shaky, "He was in the living room, newspaper on his lap, his head down. I felt relief at first. Stan was a sound sleeper and I figured he just didn't hear the phone. I laughed nervously and started talking to him. As I neared him I panicked, his skin looked so pale, so cold. I screamed his name and ran to him. I grabbed his shoulders to shake him and his hand flopped off the armrest. He was dead."

Richard felt himself getting choked up, but couldn't make any response. His heart was already going out to this poor man. Finally he found his voice, "How awful to find your lover dead!"

"Oh God," Antone' moaned, "It was too horrible to believe."

Richard stopped him, "Please, you don't need to go on. I won't let you. Such a loss is bad enough to live through, you shouldn't have to relive it."

Recovering his composure, Antone' thanked Richard and apologized for breaking down like that. "I didn't mean to go on like that. Look, I'll understand if you'd rather not meet. I come with some pretty heavy baggage."

"Don't you dare hang up!" Richard said sternly. "Everyone comes with baggage. One day I'll share mine. Where do you live? I'd like to take you out for dinner Friday night."

Antone' gave him McNaulty's address.

"Pick you up at 7:00?"

"That would be great. Thank you." Antone' said softly. "Good-bye, Richard." He hung up, holding onto the receiver for a moment as a voice warned, 'Don't.' He ignored the warning, hoisted his bag, and bounded upstairs to unpack. He refused to even hear the warning voice in his head, but it was there, and he'd have to fight it harder than ever.

Chapter 4 — DECEMBER 8th

So far, police in Dayton, Ohio, had uncovered no clues as to the whereabouts of John Ziemens, the suspected murderer of Walter Marqueth. The crime scene investigation had failed to turn up any viable clues. There were no prints, other than the victims, nor was there any hair, blood or even semen samples that were usable, and, as suspected, the name was an alias. The suspect had not been seen in any other city's gay bars, although quite a few patrons did recognize him from the composite put together the help of Judith Wilset, Marqueth's sister. He simply seemed to vanish.

"What do we do now?" Detective Ogsten asked at the morning briefing session.

Pacing the small room, Chief Myers had only one thought. "Maybe we should contact other Police Departments, find out if they've had any similar cases. This might not be an isolated incident." He stopped pacing and leaned on the desk, "Ogsten, get a teletype out with a description of this guy. Ask if they've had any similar crimes that are still unsolved."

"Right. Anything else?"

Chief Myers shook his head and Ogsten left.

If wasn't long before they got a response. It seems that police in Denver had a similar case the previous July. The death of William Stoeman, whose body was found the morning of July 6th washed up on the shore of the South Platte River, north of Denver, had been ruled an accidental drowning. According to friends, Stoeman and his young boyfriend had gone canoeing over the 4th of July weekend and failed to return home. A search was conducted, and 2 days later Stoeman's body was found. The canoe they'd rented was also found nearby, it was badly damaged from repeatedly striking rocks under the rapids and along the shore line. Stoeman's body bore many deep, jagged cuts, broken bones and bruises, the more severe being in the head area. The search continued for several more days for his boyfriend's body, but it was never found. Based on the evidence at the scene, police presumed that his body was washed down river, but the case remained open, there were unanswered questions about the young man's identity.

"Chief, look at the description in the last paragraph."

"It could be the same guy," he said, "Get a composite of our suspect and fax it to them, see if he looks anything like Stoeman's missing boyfriend."

By late afternoon they had confirmation from Denver. The composite bore a strong resemblance to Stoeman's boyfriend, but they were still fairly certain he was dead.

"Look at this," Ogsten said, pointing to the last sentence in the teletype.

"What? Where?"

"Here, his name."

"What of it?"

"Don't you think it's a bit unusual for two men, both gay, both dating older men, who either turn up dead or murdered, to have a surname that starts with the letter z?"

"Christ, you're right!" Chief Myers called his secretary, "Get me Dr. Arno. I need him to do a profile for me."

Dr. Arno, the department's criminal psychologist, arrived shortly. "You need me, Chief?"

"Yeah, Ed. I need you to do a profile for me, pronto. We may have something in the Marqueth case."

"Sure. What do you have so far.?"

Chief Myers briefly sketched out the information they had and what they'd learned from Denver.

"Now," he continued, "We're getting reports from departments in Pennsylvania, New York and Jersey claiming he's there. Denver still thinks he's dead, and we can't find hide nor hair of him. What's your take on all this?"

Dr. Arno read the description and studied the composite. "I think the biggest problem is that this guy could be one of thousands of young gay men. There's no distinguishing characteristic about him. No scars, tattoos, birthmarks, nothing that would make him stand out."

Chief Myers tented his fingers under his chin as he thought. "But he is, according to all accounts, very good looking."

Dr. Arno laughed, "Have you ever seen any of the Pride Day Parades?"

Chief Myers shook his head.

"There are many really good looking gay men, so that won't help. It would be easier if he was ugly."

Both men laughed.

"So we have nothing to go on?"

"No, not true." Swinging around beside Chief Myers, Dr. Arno pointed out a few facts. "One, both victims, I'm assuming the man in Denver was murdered by him, died on or around a holiday. Two, both were older and fairly well off. Three, neither had many siblings. Last, his last name, the use of the letter z."

"Yeah, Ogsten pointed that out to me."

"Why holidays, though? What could there be about a celebration that would make someone want to kill? Especially someone they're dating!"

"Considering all the calls we get for domestic violence around holidays, drinking comes to mind."

"That could very well be it!" Dr. Arno exclaimed as he got up.

"You think so?"

"I'm not saying for sure it is, but it's a pretty good bet."

"Okay, let's assume that's so. What connection is this guy making? I mean, why? What's going on in his head?"

Dr. Arno made some associations with the facts they had. The common thread he came up with was violence. Holidays, violence in for form of robbery, suicide and family problems. Alcohol, violence in the form of fights, shootings, and domestic problems. Older men, violence in the form of abuse. "But why," he wondered aloud as he walked over to the window, "Would a man in his early 30's pick men in their 50's, date them, probably become intimate with them, and then as a holiday approaches, kill them?" He turned away from the darkening skyline, pondering his own question, then he hit on an idea. "Abuse. More than likely he'd been physically, and probably sexually abused as a child. He could have been mocked by his abuser while he was using him. Calling him derogatory names like queer, faggot and the like."

"Hold it, Ed," Chief Myers was confused, "If this guy was having sex with him, couldn't all those names apply to him as well?"

Dr. Arno shook his head. "He probably used him as he would a prostitute. He would be dominant, not passive, so in his mind, he was still a man. Our guy was the little queer."

"So what you're telling me is that by killing older men he's getting back at that other man for what he did to him when he was a kid?"

"Not exactly. He does date these men, doesn't he?"

"Yeah, Until a holiday comes up."

"Okay. So he is attracted to older men. Probably believes they're more secure, stable."

"Like a father figure?"

"Could be. But when a holiday approaches..."

"He goes psycho and offs them." Chief Myers interrupted.

"In a crude way, yes. He fears the abuse will happen again and he has to save himself from it."

"By killing them?"

"It looks that way, if these turn out to have been done by the same guy."

"Jesus!" Chief Myers said slowly, realizing what the next holiday was. "New Year's Eve is right around the corner, and not only is it New Year's, it's the Millennium!" Looking up at Dr. Arno, he asked, "There could be multiple murders, couldn't there? I mean if this guy's in the right place, he could take out more than just one victim."

"I'm afraid that is a possibility. There are many gay couples who have a noticeable age difference. This upcoming holiday is going to be the biggest party anybody's ever seen. If he gets a mind to, you could be right. It depends on where he's heading."

"Any thoughts on that?"

"My gut reaction, based on where the two previous incidents have taken place, is a major city. He appears to be heading in an easterly direction, so maybe New York, Boston, Philadelphia, I really don't know. He could be there already and is probably with the next victim."

Chief Myers called Officer Lopez in, "I want you to get in touch with New York, Philly, Boston, even D.C. Send them a composite and tell them to be on the alert for this guy. Have them concentrate their efforts in the gay bars and any hotels, or resorts that may be in their city. Be sure to let them know that the common thread so far is that he goes for older men and that any name he uses starts with a Z." Lopez nodded and was gone.

Dr. Arno got up to leave. "One more thing, Chief. Call your son. Tell him what's going on."

Chief Myers looked confused.

"He and his lover do own a gay resort in the Poconos, don't they?"

"How do you know?"

Dr. Arno smiled as he opened the door. "I've been there, nice place. See ya, Chief." He winked and closed the door behind him.

Chief Myers was stunned.

Antone' woke in the small room at McNaulty's. He was getting restless, there was little to do to occupy his time. It was too cold to walk around, he wasn't hungry and didn't really feel like getting too friendly with Millie at DeLucas.

Pacing the small room, he caught a glimpse of himself in the mirror above the dresser. He looked good, considering, but needed a shave and a shower. He took care of those things and felt much more refreshed. Again he started the pacing. The sun had broken through and despite the cold temperatures, he decided he needed to move. Walking would help him think, clear his mind of its torments and fears. He walked down Penn Avenue, towards Market Square, admiring the city, his mood brightening a bit.

It wasn't long, however, before his mind began to cloud over, the darkness returning. His pace and breathing quickened and he began to sweat. "This is not good," he said to himself as he reached Market Square. He slowed his pace and tried to admire the holiday decorations that filled every store front and lined the streets, but each time he saw a Santa Claus, or a holiday tree, or heard a Christmas Carroll, his mind snapped back to the holidays of his childhood.

He had no idea how far he had walked, but he turned around and started back. The sky was beginning to darken and the temperature drop even more. By the time he got to DeLucas, he was exhausted and hungry. He looked in, didn't see Millie, and decided to get something to eat.

The McNaulty's were watching television in the living room when he returned. "Would you like to join us?" Mrs. McNaulty asked.

"No, thank you," Antone' replied, "I took a long walk today and I'm freezing. I'd like to take a hot bath, if that's all right."

"Of course. Are you hungry?"

"I ate at DeLucas just before. I would like a book, or magazine to read, though."

Mrs. McNaulty pointed to a book case along the far wall, "Help yourself."

Antone' selected a novel of an author he'd never heard of and, thanking them, said good night and went up to his room. Once inside he tossed the book on the chair and fell onto the bed. His heart will still pounding, he could hear it, and try as he might, he couldn't erase the tape that ran through his head in a continuous loop. He quickly got up, grabbed the book and headed to the bathroom. Filling the tub with water as hot as he could stand it, he sank in and opened the book. He forced himself to concentrate on the words as the hot water warmed and calmed him. "Better," he thought, and felt himself regaining control of the situation. But the darkness was still there, how long he could control it he didn't know.

Chapter 5 — DECEMBER 9th

Charlie was busy in the small office off the lobby in the main lodge. Having completed November's ledger, he turned his attention to what would be their major money maker of the year, New Year's Eve. They had kept the tradition of the previous owners, a 3 day, 2 night stay that included 2 meals a day, with a special menu on New Year's Eve. Also included in the package deal was free admission to the disco, and on the night of the big event, hats, noisemakers, a champagne toast at midnight followed by a buffet.

This being their first major event as owners, as well as the millennium, they had to do something special. Early in the spring they had tossed around several ideas. Male strippers, 'No, too overdone,' a drag show, 'Oh please! Not again,' a celebrity, 'Right. Who?' Charlie had made calls to friends and associates in Manhattan, fishing for ideas and possible leads, but nothing turned up. Memorial Day came and went without a big name attraction.

The day after Memorial Day, Tina, one of the chefs, came to Charlie with an idea.

"My girlfriend and I were in New Hope over the weekend, and we went to the Cartwheel. They had a group entertaining there. They were really good. I spoke to the manager of the group afterwards and got their card. She handed it to Charlie. 'NuView Review', it read, Harold Morgan Manager, along with a Philadelphia phone number.

"What kind of a show do they put on?" Charlie asked, still looking at the plain printed card.

"It's kind of like the old Vandeville shows, a variety show. Some singing, live, not lip-sinc. Skits, stand-up comedy. Some drag, but it's all good. The Cartwheel was packed and everyone loved them."

"Did you find out where else they've performed?"

Tina nodded, "Resorts in Atlantic City, Actor's Playhouse in the Village, Marlin Beach Hotel in Lauderdale, and some other places I can't remember. Harold said he'd send a brief video of their act if you'd like."

"Sounds good. I'll give him a call right now. Thanks, Tina, this could be what we're looking for. I just hope they're not too expensive."

"That I don't know, but..." her voice trailed off.

"I guess I'll find out soon enough," Charlie said as he reached for the phone.

Tina got up to leave the office.

"Thanks again, Tina," Charlie called as he began dialing the number. She smiled and left, closing the office door behind her.

A sleepy voice answered the phone of the fourth ring. "Is this Harold Morgan?"

"Speaking," he croaked, clearing his throat. Harold continued, "Who is calling, please?"

"My name is Charlie Burtram, one of the owners of Lambda Lodge and Resort in the Poconos."

"Yes, Mr. Burtram, how can I help you?" Harold asked, forcing himself awake.

"One of my employees, Tina Cuthberg, caught your show at the Cartwheel this past weekend and spoke to you about possibly performing for us over New Year's."

"You'll forgive me if I don't quite remember her, but yes, someone did speak to me about a booking for New Year's. It could have been her. We're not booked anywhere yet. As a matter of fact we've been debating if we want to perform at all, this being the millennium and all."

"I see," Charlie was disappointed. "Do you think you'd consider spending the New Year here at our lodge?"

Harold nodded, he was interested. "We can discuss it. You're in the Poconos, aren't you?"

"That's right, on Mt. Nebo. It's quiet and restful here," Charlie began selling Harold on the idea, "You'd have your rooms and meals provided, and time to enjoy the holiday and relax. We'd only want you to do two shows. You'd be as much of a guest as anyone else."

"You do make it sound tempting. Let's talk more, you've got me interested."

They talked for another half-hour or more about the facilities, type of show they do and the most important item, the cost. The fee was a bit more than Charlie had anticipated, then Harold told him, "We donate 10% of our fee to A.I.D.S. charities in the cities we perform in, so you'd be doing a service for your own community, as well as getting a quality show." Now Harold was selling.

"You know what, this sounds good to me, but if I book you without talking to my other half, I'll be divorced before you get here. Why don't we tentatively book it, you send the video and I'll talk to Jonathan."

They set the dates, and discussed any special needs of the group and after a few minutes more, hung up. Charlie felt good about this. They seemed to be a popular group, had a wide range of talent, and more importantly, Charlie liked Harold, he was up front and personable. Charlie went into the kitchen, found Tina, and kissed her on the forehead.

Tina burst into a wide grin, "You booked them! How great! You won't be disappointed, I promise you."

"Right now," Charlie cautioned her, "It's tentative. Harold's sending their video, and I have to talk to Jonathan. But it looks good."

The kitchen was buzzing, everyone wanted to share in the excitement. Charlie filled them in on the news. "I've seen them, they are good," responded Frank, one of the waiters, "Good goin', Tina."

"When will you know for sure?" Tina asked.

Heading towards the door, Charlie said, "As soon as I talk to Jonathan."

By the end of the next week the deal had been finalized. Harold sent a stack of the groups' fliers to be mailed with the lodge's next newsletter, along with reservation forms and price list for the three different buildings. Now, December 8th, they were booked solid, had been since early in the fall. People were still calling for reservations, but the best they could do was put them on a waiting list.

Charlie looked out of the office window. The pristine snow lie deep under a crystalline blue sky. The row of cabins sat silent, dark, and cold. "If only they were heated," he thought aloud, "Maybe next year."

"I still can't believe we have a booking for New Year's Eve!" complained Ron DuBuois, the newest member of NuView Review. "I was really looking forward to spending the entire holiday season with my family and friends."

Watching him pace around Harold's small apartment living room in down town Philadelphia was making Anthony nervous. Finally, he could bear it no longer. He got up, and taking him by the shoulders, sat Ron on the couch. "Will you please calm down! There's nothing you can do about it now, all the arrangements were made months ago. Besides, it's not like you won't be able to spend some time at home. We don't have to be there until the 29th, so Christmas is all yours. We're only doing 2 performances over the 3-day stay, our rooms are provided, meals are gratis, and they're paying a premium price. Harold is giving each of us a nice bonus to boot, so relax, will you?" Anthony smiled a sly smile, "And who knows, maybe you'll finally meet the man of your dreams."

At that, Ron had to laugh, and the tension was broken. "I guess if you put it that way, it'll be okay. You always know how to get to me don't you?"

Getting up from the couch, a smug look on his face, Anthony simply said, "I'm good, aren't I? Now, with that finally settled for the thousandth time, let's do some rehearsing, Harold and the rest of the guys will be back soon, and I don't feel like hearing Harold bitch any more." Extending a hand to Ron to pull him up, he finished, "Your finale needs to be polished up anyway." Ron rolled his eyes as Anthony pulled him to his feet.

The popularity of NuView stemmed from its variety. Harold had done stand up comedy for years, and when he added drag to it, transforming himself into Ethel Merman, his act became an outrageous success. Ray Coleman did some song and dance, as well as brief comedy skits, reminiscent of Vaudeville. Anthony Deangelo was the consummate crooner, and being part Latino and Italian with the dark hair and deep mysterious eyes made men, women, and butch lesbians swoon, especially when he dressed in a tux. Ron came on board early last spring, he brought magic and the art of illusion to the group. He had done some drag, but found it mundane and uncomfortable, he swore he'd never do it again. When Harold saw a photo of Ron in full drag, however, he gasped. Ron could be Ann Margaret's double! Immediately he started thinking of how to incorporate that image into Ron's segments of the show. Late one night, unable to sleep, Harold turned on the television. An old Bible movie was on, he loved those, they were so camp. Suddenly, staring at the screen, he shouted, "That's it!"

The next day he approached Ron with the idea. He was hesitant at first, but Harold was persistent, and finally convinced him by saying, "It will be your finest illusion, not drag!"

Slowly a smile appeared on Ron's face, "Yeah, I see what you mean. Okay, I'll do it!"

This segment of the act became such a hit it was used as the finale, nobody left the audience until Ron did his seductive, sensuous striptease. The costume consisted of layers of veils made of sheer organza, in various shades of blue. He'd swirl, strut, and play coy with the audience, slowly peeling off veil after veil. The blue lighting used for this number gave the act a distant, surreal look. Ron took his time, heightening the effect of the illusion. By the time he was left wearing a few veils and his bra and panties, smoke from the dry ice machine surrounded him and rose in wisps to his neck. As the smoke thickened and engulfed him, he'd remove the remaining veils and play shy with the audience, holding the bra, pretending not to want to finish, but when the smoke was high enough, he'd unhook and remove the bra, revealing himself, mostly unseen, to the anxious audience. The lights would instantly go out, and he would seem to evaporate into the smoke. Many people swore it was a woman, others had no idea. It was his finest illusion, and sure to be a hit at Lambda Lodge.

Chapter 6 — DECEMBER 10th

Richard arrived at McNaulty's shortly after 7:00. Antone', known to him as Paul, was waiting in the small living room. From his broad smile and hearty handshake, it was obvious that Richard was pleased with what he saw. Antone's dark, wavy hair, green eyes, and beautifully trim body comprised quite an attractive package. Antone' smiled back at Richard and asked him in for a moment, but Richard declined saying that he'd made reservations at

1902 Landmark Tavern, on Market Square, and that they'd better get going. A look of concern clouded Antone's face, "Am I dressed okay?" he asked. Richard gladly surveyed Antone' again.

"You look great from where I stand. Let's go."

The drive to the restaurant was filled with conversation and laughter. At one point, Antone' reached over and squeezed Richard's thigh, then quickly pulled back. Glancing sideways at him, Richard smiled, "Don't pull away, that felt rather nice." Antone' returned his hand, it was quickly grasped and held by Richard. They drove the rest of the short distance in silence.

"Well, we're here," Richard said as he parked his Town Car along the curb.

Antone' looked at the building, "Wow, this place must be old."

"That it is. Come on, I'll tell you about it when we get inside, it's freezing out here."

When they entered the restaurant, Antone' noticed a distinct aroma. Noticing this, Richard told him that there had been a raw bar just as you walked in, but it was removed about 6 weeks ago. Too "fragrant".

As they walked through the tiled entry, Antone's attention was drawn to the photos along the wall. "Those were taken some time in the 1920's or 1930's I believe. Here, look at this one." The photo Richard pointed to had captured the original owners, the Dimling brothers. "This used to be their restaurant and, believe it or not, bait shop."

"Bait shop!" Antone' laughed, "You've got to be kidding!"

"Nope, that's what it was. Of course, it's been solely a restaurant for many years now. The current owners bought it sometime in the 1980's and restored it a great deal."

As they entered the main dining room, Antone's attention was drawn to the beautifully carved mahogany bar that lined one side of the room. "That thing is huge!" he remarked.

"It is something else, isn't it? If I'm correct, it was bought somewhere in central Pennsylvania and relocated here. I love the wood, it's so rich and warm."

"It is," Antone' replied, walking up to it and running his hand on the smooth aged wood, "I like it."

Richard smiled, glad that he thought of this place for their first date.

"Can I get you gentlemen anything?" the bartender asked. Richard ordered a glass of Burgundy, Antone' got a coke. As they drank, Antone's eyes wandered around the room. The walls were wooden, mahogany again, and mirrored. The lighting fixtures were all brass, and added a rich glow to the wood. You felt comfortable here, drawn in by the ambiance of the decor and the history of the building itself. The windows in front looked out onto Market Square itself decorated now in holiday splendor. Antone' glanced out, but looked immediately away, remembering the darkness he had felt earlier in the week. True, the restaurant itself was decorated for the holidays, but as long as he kept his attention on Richard and on the conversation, he felt he'd be all right.

When they'd finished their drinks, Richard asked to be seated. At first the hostess led them to a table near the window, but Antone' asked Richard if they could sit at one of the booths along the far wall, behind the end of the bar. When Richard asked why, Antone' said he'd be too cold sitting near the windows. The hostess reseated them.

"This is better," Antone' smiled and looked around the room. It was decorated with red, white and pink poinsettias, and a live balsam holiday tree strung with small, clear mini-lights. From the din in the room, it was obvious people were getting excited about the upcoming holidays. Antone' tried to tune out the bits and pieces he overheard by reading the menu.

"The food here is quite good, and reasonable," Richard said, "Do you see anything you like?"

Antone' grinned, then laughed.

"On the menu I meant!" Richard countered, laughing himself, "But thank you for the compliment."

"You're quite welcome. And, yes, I do see something I like on the menu as well. I think I'll try the sea scallops, they sound good. How about you?"

"I'm going to have the pork chops. I know they're good here."

"You eat here often, then?" Antone' asked, sipping water.

"About once every 2 weeks or so. I usually do my own cooking, but it gets lonely and sometimes I just need to get out and be with people."

As Antone' listened, he found himself staring into Richard's eyes, they were such a pale blue they were almost colorless, and sparkled even in the dim light of the restaurant. His close cropped salt and pepper hair framed his rugged, angular face perfectly. He wore no jewelry on his big hands, as so many older gay men did, and they moved strongly as he spoke, no effeminate waving. His voice was deep and resonant. He was a man who was comfortable with himself and who he was. Antone' found himself relaxing and, for once, being right here in the moment.

"Are you gentlemen ready to order?" The waitress's voice snapped Antone' back. They placed their orders, and had a second round of drinks. Shortly, their salads and a basket of warm, crusty French bread arrived.

"So, Paul, how did you end up here in Pittsburgh?"

Antone' continued his fabrication from earlier in the week. "I couldn't stay in the house long after Stan's funeral. His sister was the sole heir and had put it up for sale. A few friends had offered to let me stay with them, and I did, but only for a short while. Everything seemed to be closing in around me. The house was sold quickly, and seeing new people move in and all of our things being either sold at an auction, or given to relatives was too much for me to bear. I had to get out. Stan's sister never approved of me, always thought I was with Stan for his money, so I got almost nothing from the estate. I took what little I had, packed up, closed out my checking and small savings accounts, even sold my car, and boarded a bus. I has hoping to find work here in banking or as an accountant."

"Why not go home? Surely your family would have helped you out."

Antone' stopped, his fork in mid-air, "Oh no! Not to that little spit of a town. I wanted to improve my situation, not descend farther. There was nothing there for me. My parents begged me to come back, 'just until you decide what you want to do,' but I knew that if I went back I'd never get out again."

"Accounting, huh?" Richard sat back and crossed his arms, "Let me see what I can do. I know some people."

Antone' immediately protested, "Richard, you don't need to do that. I'd feel guilty, like I was using you. We just met, and if you get me a job and it doesn't work out I don't want people blaming you, or you getting angry with me."

"Paul, don't be ridiculous," Richard countered, now leaning forward to emphasize his point, "I'll give you names of firms I know, you apply, use my name as a reference. If they hire you it will be on your own merit, not because of me. Is that all right?"

Antone' smiled, "Yeah, that I could live with."

Their meals arrived, full of wonderful aromas, and flavor. Taking his first bite, Antone' looked up at Richard and winked.

Suddenly, a dark flash clouded his eyes, 'What are you doing? You know what he is.'

"Paul, is everything all right?"

"Yes. I'm sorry, I just got a little dizzy there. I haven't been eating very much since I got into town."

"We can't have that happening any more. Do you need money? I can lend you some until you get a job."

"No, I'm fine. Really. Thank you though, that was sweet of you to offer."

"Your welcome. Now eat, and don't forget to order a dessert. They have wonderful cakes here."

Antone' returned to his meal, fighting the dark, nagging voice that insisted on being heard.

Chapter 7 — DECEMBER 15th

"Dad! Hi. What's up?" Jonathan was a bit surprised by his father's call. Their relationship was best described as cordial. Jonathan's parents had divorced when he was 8 or 9 years old. Their marriage had deteriorated as the demands of his police work increased. With his advancement from an officer to detective, Jonathan's father began searching for something more, a place to challenge him. The Poconos were relatively quiet from a law enforcement point of view. He felt restless and bored. Myers and his wife began arguing more frequently, she wanted to remain in East Stroudsburg where she felt safe and settled, he wanted more excitement and challenge. The offer of Chief of Police in Dayton, Ohio, was the breaking point. Mrs. Myers wouldn't move, she couldn't let her son be raised in a 'city', a dirty word for her. Myers tried to reason with her, pointing out advantages such as museums, theater, better schools. She countered with increased crime, possible drug involvement, and exposure to gangs. It was a stalemate.

"What do we do now?" he asked her late one night as they sat at the kitchen table.

"I think we both know the answer to that question," she calmly replied, staring at her clasped hands.

"Yeah, I guess we do. I love you, but wish you'd give this a chance. Be more adventurous."

Still staring at her hands, she slowly shook her head. "No, I can't. I need to stay here. My life is here." Finally looking up at him, her eyes imploring, she concluded, "I wish you were more content."

He got up, and rubbing the back of his neck, ended the conversation and their marriage. "I guess that's always been the biggest problem between us. What do we tell Jonathan?"

She wiped the tears that had suddenly appeared on her face, "Well, we could tell him you're going to try a new job and that you'll be away for a while," she smiled at him, "Who knows, you might hate it and be back in a month or so."

He chuckled at her optimism.

That was 27 years ago.

Jonathan slowly grew to realize the reality of the situation. Shortly before his 10th birthday he angrily blurted out, "Daddy's never coming back, is he?" his face scrunched into a tearful pout, "The kids say you're divorced!"

"Come here, honey," she held out her arms to him, her heart breaking. Curling up in her lap she explained, as best she could, the situation. When she'd finished he asked only one question, "Will I ever see daddy again?"

She could only cry, nod her head and hold him closer.

By the time he was 15, Jonathan's life as a child of a broken home seemed okay. He had his mom's full attention during the school year in the Poconos, and his dad's during the summer visits and the holidays he spent in Dayton. However the summer before his 16th birthday changed this amicable relationship forever.

Myers had returned home early one day, and upon opening the back door, heard laughter and giggling coming from the basement den. Thinking nothing of it at first, he grabbed a beer out of the refrigerator. Passing the open basement door on the way to the living room, he heard a few gasps and whispers, "God that feels good!" He froze. Listening intently now, he heard more, "Ooh, yeah, do that again." Thinking his son was with some high school girl, he raced down the carpeted stairs. He was dumbfounded to see his son with another boy, naked and groping each other on the den floor. His head swirled and he screeched, "What the hell are you two doing! You!" he pointed to the humiliated youth, "Get out! Now!" Both boys had already started scrambling into their shorts and T-shirts. The terrified boy grabbed his sneakers and fled up the stairs, past the irate Myers like a blur, the back door slamming shut behind him.

Jonathan, already dressed, sat on the edge of the couch, staring at the floor, biting his nails. Myers stood frozen, his breathing hard and fast, glaring at his son. Finally, his trembling knees gave out and he sank onto the stairs. In his 7 or 8 years here in Dayton, he had seen his share of gays, they were the brunt of many jokes in the office, mockingly mimicked by officers. To him, and many others in law enforcement, they were all limp wristed swishes. Now, his son! His only child! No, it was too much to bear. He was beyond anger, hurt and shock. He slowly got up, and in a voice that came from somewhere else, heard himself say, "Go to your room and pack, "You're going back to your mother tonight."

By now, Jonathan had calmed down a little, but his father's order to leave cut so deeply he burst into tears, "Dad!'

"Don't. Don't say a word!" his father interrupted in a seething voice, "I can't talk to you now. Maybe later, much later. But before I say anything at all, I want you to leave." Jonathan heard his father's heavy footsteps on the stairs as Myers numbly walked back through the kitchen and into the living room, where he finally opened the beer he was still clutching.

Jonathan silently crept up from the den and tiptoed through the living room. He stopped at the bottom of the stairs and turned to his father, "Dad, please..." Myers turned on the television in response. Jonathan fled up the stairs.

An hour or so later he came back down, suitcase in hand. His father was still sitting in the living room, motionless. Not only had he finished that first beer, but several others as well. Seeing this made

Jonathan angry, "How am I going to get home?" he asked coldly.

His father handed him a slip of paper, it had a flight number and departure time written on it. "You can use your original return ticket," he said flatly.

"Are you going to drive me to the airport?"

Myers looked at the beer in his hand, and the several empty cans on the end table, "If I drove now, I'd be arrested for D.W.I., and I've had quite enough to deal with today."

Dropping his bags, Jonathan sharply replied, "Fine, I'll call a cab, but I'll need money."

Without looking at him, Myers told Jonathan to take what he needed from his wallet on the kitchen table.

Jonathan placed the call then made himself a sandwich, and ate it over the kitchen sink. Shortly, he heard a car honking. He picked up his bags and started walking to the front door. "That's my cab. Bye, Dad," Jonathan started approaching his father to hug him as he had done countless times over the years, but Myers pulled away. Jonathan felt tears again, but fought them back. He opened the door, then turned back, "You know, no matter what I am there's one thing that will never change. I'll always be your son!" he said through clenched teeth. "You'd better call Mom and tell her I'm on my way home." He slammed out of the house, and, he thought, his father's life.

The next time Jonathan saw his father was at high school graduation a few years later. Their reunion was friendly, no great explosion of emotion, but the door to rebuilding a relationship was open.

That autumn, Jonathan started his college career at Penn State, in Happy Valley. Here he found a very active gay community, and his first boyfriend. His mother, although somewhat surprised when be brought Ted home for a visit and told her he was gay, admitted that she always thought he was. She also told him that his father had a great deal of trouble dealing with it.

"I wish Dad could have been as understanding as you've been. I'm still the same person I always was, this doesn't change me. How did you know?"

Mrs. Myers simply shrugged and replied, "Mother's intuition. Honey, don't worry about your father, he'll come around. You remember the night he threw you out?"

"How could I forget that night!"

"When he called me to say he were on your way home and that he wasn't going to be able to have you visit 'for a while', as he put it, he cried his eyes out. I'd never heard him cry like that before. He was hurt, and shocked, probably still is in a way," she held his hands, "But he loves you very much."

Jonathan squeezed his mother's hands in his, "I know, I just wish things could be better between us," he kissed her hands. "So, what do you think of Ted?" They both laughed.

Jonathan's relationship with his father recovered a bit more over the next few years. At his ex-wife's urging, Myers educated himself about homosexuality, and discovered some surprising facts; like the possibility that it's genetic, that many men deny their sexuality, get married, and even father children while sneaking around to adult bookstores for male sex, even that some sports figures are gay. He became more sensitive to what were now being called 'hate crimes' against gays and lesbians. He tried to set up seminars for his officers, but met resistance and outright anger.

After several months of futile efforts to have officers volunteer to attend these meetings, he'd had enough. One morning, after roll call, he brought the issue up and got the expected response. This time he let his anger get the best of him. "You guys kill me!" he shouted, "Look at yourselves, are you afraid it's contagious? Or that someone will think you're gay if you attend these seminars?"

Turning their own prejudice back on them, he looked squarely at Officer Lopez, "Hector, how do you feel when you hear people call you a spick?" Lopez's dark Latino eyes flashed. Myers continued, "And you, Washington, how does nigger grab you?"

"Now wait a minute, Chief!" Washington yelled, standing up to all of his 6'4" frame.

Reacting quickly, Myers looked up into Washington's angry eyes, "No! You wait a minute," his eyes swept the room, "All of you!" The room became silent as Washington, Lopez, and the rest of the officers squirmed uncomfortably. "Many of you have been called something derogatory. Some of your people have been beaten, even killed because of their race or ethnic background. These people are being beaten, harassed, fired from their jobs, denied housing because of their sexual orientation. We've all mocked them. Haven't we?" There was a low murmur of guilt. "Well those days are over. We're here to protect and serve everyone," he emphasized the last word, "Do I make myself clear?"

Knowing they were defeated, the officers grudgingly agreed. The seminars would begin within a week and run for a period of 3 weeks. Attendance was mandatory, miss a session, you make it up. Myers dismissed the men and women, and started to his office. Officer Adams stopped him, "Chief, why are you being so tough on this issue? You never liked or defended fags, I mean gays before, Why now?"

77

"You remember what happened in Wyoming last November? That 19 year old boy beaten and then hung on a barbed wire fence to die!"

Hanging his head, Adams whispered that he did.

"That got to me, but the thing that really made me turn the corner on this issue was that there were protesters at his funeral! For God's sake, the kid was murdered, and people were there taunting his family and friends! And," Myers raised a finger, driving home his next point, "The worst part was that these morons were being led by some ass of a minister! A man of God! That was more than I could take. I don't know what God he serves, but it sure as hell isn't the one I pray to." He put his hands in his pockets, "Any more questions?"

Officer Adams was speechless, he simply shook his head and turned away.

Now, several years later, he was calling his son to warn him about the possibility of a serial killer heading his way. After telling Jonathan about the two known victims, and the likelihood of others, he said he wanted to send flyers to him for distribution throughout the Pocono area. "Could you do that for me?"

"Of course I can, Dad. You don't really think this guy would show up here in the mountains, do you?"

Sighing, Myers told him he just didn't know where this guy could be heading, "So far, he's only struck in major cities, but both known murders happened around holidays, and I'm sure you'll have a large crowd this New Year's Eve. I want you and your guests to be safe."

"Dad, that's really great of you. Thanks. I'll be sure to distribute the flyers as soon as they get here. We have a mailing list of all the gay establishments in the area. Do you have a description yet?"

"Yeah, but it's sketchy. Dark hair and eyes, attractive, in his early 30's. That's about it. He seems to prefer older men, but that's not a hardened fact. I just don't want you hurt. Like you told me so long ago, 'You'll always be my son.' Bye Jonathan."

"Bye, Dad," Jonathan choked through tears.

Myers hung up and rubbed his face. He was concerned for his son, any parent would be, but he also felt guilt and shame for his reaction to his son's homosexuality so many years ago. He was going to be sure this guy was caught before anyone else got hurt.

Detective Ogsten came through the open door, "Chief, I think we might have just found another victim."

Myers felt is heart sink, "Oh, no. Where?" he got up, extending his hand to take the sheet of paper Ogsten was holding out to him.

"We got a teletype from Chicago. It seems that they had a similar case over Labor Day weekend. The details are sketchy, but much of their finds fit with what happened here and in Denver."

Myers scanned the page, "This does sound all too familiar."

The teletype from Chicago contained information on the possible murder of James Orgel. His description was similar to those of Marqueth's and

Stoeman's. The events before his death were too much like the others to be a coincidence.

"You know," Myers said, "I've been thinking about the aliases he uses, all starting with a Z. It's as if he's telling his victims that he's the end of the line for them."

"Eerie, isn't it?"

"Yeah. Well, it looks as if our worst fears have been realized. We've got a serial killer on our hands."

Chapter 8 — DECEMBER 18th

Antone' slipped off his shoes and propped his feet up on the coffee table in Richard's study. He told Richard that he was not having any luck finding a job, nobody was hiring this late in the year. In truth, the only jobs he'd applied for were the ones that Richard had helped him get interviews for, the rest he fabricated based on those experiences. He'd spent most of the day cruising Point State Park, wasting time.

Richard, unaware of these facts, had treated him wonderfully, thinking that this is a young man who he could fall for a build a life with. He'd treated Antone' to dinner, movies, and shopping for some new clothes, offering to pay for everything, but being rebuked. Antone' still had a sizable amount of cash left, and wasn't about to let Richard pay for him, at least not yet.

As they sat in front of the roaring fire, sipping brandy, Richard pulled him close and kissed him, "I've wanted to do that since the moment I laid eyes on you," he whispered, stroking Antone's face gently.

"Why did you wait so long?"

Leaning back on the overstuffed sofa, Richard explained, "Being an older man and still alone, I've developed a bit of a protective wall, especially when it comes to dating younger men. Most of them are looking for someone to take care of them, to keep them. I've seen it happen to some of my friends. They've been used, hurt, taken for money and jewelry, then abandoned."

Putting his arm around Richard and resting his head on his chest, Antone' softly asked, "Is that what you thought I'd do?"

Kissing him on the head, Richard nodded, "At first, but you've barely taken a dime from me, you sent me those beautiful flowers," he motioned to the bouquet of red roses and white daisies on the mantle, "And have been nothing but a sweet, loving person."

Richard reached for an envelope on the end table. "Now I have something for you, a sort of Christmas present." He handed the envelope to Antone'. A puzzled look came over his face, "Richard, I..."

Sushing him, Richard said, "Paul, please just open the envelope."

He did as asked, "This is a reservation form. What are you doing?"

Richard simply instructed him to read on.

Antone's eyes widened and his jaw dropped. "You're taking me here for New Year's?"

Laughing like a young boy, Richard said, "I take it your pleased."

"Pleased!" Antone' exclaimed, kissing Richard, "No one has ever done anything like this for me before! Yes, I'm pleased, I'm thrilled. Thank you." He leaned forward and kissed Richard deeply.

When the kiss ended, Richard held his face gently, "You are very welcome."

They made love for the first time that night.

Later, with Richard gently snoring beside him, Antone' lie awake, unable to sleep. He slid out of bed and pulled on his jeans. He quietly tip-toed through the dark, unfamiliar house, returning to the den. Embers still glowed in the fireplace and he stirred them a bit, then added a few small logs. As the fire flickered back to life, Antone' sat on the edge of the sofa rocking. His eyes had a tormented look, they darted side to side. His breathing was shallow and labored, and he was sheathed in sweat. Thoughts, flashes of the past pierced his mind. Snapshots etched there forever. As the kaleidoscope of visions continued, he winced and twitched, his body feeling the pain, hearing the foul words over and over again. He put his head in his hands and began mumbling. "Stop it, please stop it," he pleaded.

'No', he heard, 'You know what he'll do. They've all done it to you before, passed you around like a common whole. He'll do it too.'

"No, I don't think Richard is like the rest. He won't hurt me."

The response hissed through his head, 'They're all the same, you know that. Just like your step-father, just like your parish priest, just like...'

"Enough!" Antone' screamed. His body was trembling, hot tears streaked his flushed face.

A light came on and he heard Richard's voice calling him, "Paul! Paul what's wrong?" he called as he rushed to Antone's side, "You look terrified! My God, you're soaking wet" he exclaimed as he took Antone' in his arms, "What on earth happened?"

Allowing himself to be held, still sitting rigidly, Antone' weakly replied, "A dream, an awful dream."

"Was it about Stan?"

Antone' nodded, beginning to sob again, "It was so real. I was back in the house, and..." he broke down in Richard's arms.

Holding him tighter, Richard stroked his damp, matted hair and soothed him, "It'll be okay. You'll see. No one will hurt you now, you're with me."

Antone' closed his eyes and tried to erase the voice he had just fought. It was persistent, 'That's what they all say. You'll see, he'll turn on you. They all do.'

After another week or so of refining, rehearsing and polishing their acts, the members of NuView prepared to go their separate ways for Christmas. Before they left, however, they took time to celebrate the holiday together. They got together at Harold's apartment for dinner and to exchange gifts. Later on that night, they went out to some of the many bars in Philly. Shortly after midnight, Harold said good-night, leaving the others at Woody's. Ray and Steve soon followed, both having to catch flights to their respective homes for the holiday. Ron and Anthony sat at the downstairs bar, sipping their drinks. Ron was in no hurry to leave, he liked Anthony's company. He was hoping the feeling was mutual, but couldn't pick up any signs from Anthony's behavior. They sat in silence for a long while, Ron growing more uncomfortable by the minute. He was about to leave when Anthony put his hand on his thigh and squeezed it. "Do you mind?" he asked.

Taking Anthony's hand in his own, he said he didn't mind at all. They stayed for another drink, and spent some time talking, getting to know each other on a more personal level. Finally they left. On the way home, Ron couldn't stop thinking about Anthony. Could there be something developing between them? He surely hoped so, Anthony was one of the kindest, most open men he'd ever met. There was something about him that automatically drew Ron to him. Sure, he was gorgeous, but it went deeper than that. Ron found himself smiling the entire way home, fantasizing what life with Anthony could be like. He was determined to find out if these thoughts could become reality, but he'd have to wait until after the holidays.

Detective Ogsten had spent most of that Friday in his office accessing information from the National Crime Information Center, (NCIC). He'd started his search for clues to the true identify of John Ziemens by checking through their criminal history file without any positive leads. From there he pulled up the wanted persons file, still nothing. He checked for stolen vehicles, stolen articles, guns, securities hoping that something would turn up belonging to one of the now three victims. He met a dead end at every turn.

"Nothing. There is nothing on this guy," he told Myers at the end of the day. "How the hell is he able to keep so anonymous? It's like he doesn't even exist!"

"He doesn't."

"What? He's already committed three murders and is probably planning a fourth."

"The man we're looking for, John Ziemens, doesn't exist. The real murderer is out there, we just don't know who he really is, yet. He'll screw up, sooner or later they all do."

Ogsten loosened his tie and sat in the arm chair across from the Chief's desk, "I don't know. Either he's real good, or we're real bad. Did we miss something in the initial investigation? Is there some obvious clue sitting there, or even here in the file, waiting for us to realize it's there?"

"I don't think so," Myers said as he looked out at the setting sun.

"Then how is he getting away with it?"

Myers turned to face his Detective, "He isn't like other serial killers. He doesn't kill often. There's a very distinct motivation behind his killings, Ed pointed that out to me. We're looking for a man who's been abused, raped and humiliated at the hands of older men. Revenge can be pretty strong motivator, and in his case he's had years to prepare for it."

"What I don't get is why all of a sudden? He goes along, living his life for years then, wham! He starts killing men? It doesn't make sense to me."

Myers paced his office listening to Ogsten, and thinking at the same time. "Maybe, and this is pure conjecture at this point, but just maybe his attraction to older men developed recently, over the past few years. That attraction could have rekindled the memories of abuse he suffered years ago."

"Could be, but I don't know, Chief. It just doesn't sit right with me. There had to be some other trigger for him. Something more recent than childhood abuse. No?"

"Maybe, but right now it's all we have to go on. We're going to need help with this one."

Ogsten stood, "Yeah, I know."

Myers slapped him on the back, "Come on, let's grab a bite. We won't be able to do anything until Monday morning anyway."

Chapter 9 — DECEMBER 20th

Ron packed and boarded the Amtrak Express to Chicago early Monday morning. His family lived just south of the Windy City, in Beecher, Illinois. By air the trip would have taken just a little over an hour and a half, but Ron refused to fly unless it was unavoidable, like over water. The rest of the members of NuView thought he was being paranoid, but growing up near O'Hare Airport, he'd seen his share of plane wrecks, especially in winter.

He took a seat in the last car of the train, 'safer here', he reasoned, and got comfortable. As usual, he'd brought a book and some snacks. Since he would be traveling most of the day he thought he might even get a little shut eye, but he must have been more anxious than he thought for he found it difficult to sleep or even read at first. Knowing he wanted to be rested when he arrived home he opened his knapsack, and after finding the bottle, popped 2 Tylenol P.M., washing them down with some bottled water. He closed his eyes and was asleep within 20 minutes.

The train pulled into Chicago's depot early that afternoon, the cold air and brisk wind waking Ron instantly as he disembarked. He scanned the platform, looking for his mom and dad, not here. Starting towards the waiting room to call them, he heard his name being called, turning around he saw a hand waving frantically above the crowd. "Who the hell?" he thought aloud. Then it dawned on him and he shouted and waved back, "Jules! Jules!" It was his kid sister, he'd forgotten that she had her driver's license now.

Several hugs and kisses later they headed out to the car and home. On the way, Julie filled him in on the latest family intrigue. Their cousin Stuart's daughter got pregnant, at 16, Aunt Carol's 2nd husband lost his job and has been on a drinking binge ever since, and nobody's talking about where Uncle Lou is. Where else? Jail, probably for selling drugs. Their immediate family was large, Mr. DuBuois had 8 brothers and sisters, Mrs. DuBuois had 9 siblings. When you added spouses, children, their spouses, etcetera, you ended up with enough people to populate a small mid-west town. After hearing all this, Ron laughed and sighed, "God, I lead a boring life!"

The small, modest ranch style house was just as Ron remembered it. Built after World War II for returning G.I.'s, of which his dad was one, it had been meticulously maintained. "You put down roots, and grow from there," his father had always said, and they'd done just that. He and Julie were born and raised there, his folks retired there, and now they were growing old there.

Mrs. DuBuois was waiting at the front door wearing her brightly colored floral robe and old, worn slippers, looking as plump, red-cheeked, and Irish as ever. She saw the car and started to the driveway, waving her ample arms wildly. Ron jumped from the passenger's seat and was instantly engulfed in his mother's embrace. Julie unloaded his bags and watched their reunion, smiling through teary eyes.

"Come on, Mom, get inside. You'll catch pneumonia being out here dressed like this."

"Oh!" she exclaimed, brushing off the comment with a wave of her arm, "I've got enough blubber on me to live through an Arctic winter." They began walking towards the house, Julie carrying his bags.

Mr. DuBuois was standing in the living room, tall and as thin as ever, puffing away on the cherry blend in his pipe. "Well, the vagabond child returns," he quipped, trying to look stern.

"Hi ya, Dad," Ron warmly responded and quickly walked into his father's open arms. "It's good to see you Pop. You look great!"

"Well, your mother keeps me hoppin' around here. 'Henry, do this. Henry, do that. Henry, take me shopping.'"

"Oh, sush you," Mrs. DeBuois said as she walked past him lovingly slapping him on the arm, "Keepin' busy keeps you young." Turning to Ron, she said, "Come on, son, I'll make us something to eat, and you can fill us in on all your adventures. Besides, you're too thin anyway."

Ron looked back at Julie and they both rolled their eyes, "She'll never change," Julie commented.

"I hope not."

Most of the next day was spent shopping. Ron hadn't wanted to lug Christmas presents with him on the train, and besides, Chicago had stores that offered a wonderful variety of gifts from all around the world. They were exhausted upon returning home. Julie put up water for tea, no coffee in his house, and Ron took his packages to his old room to wrap.   After dinner they settled in the small living room, or front room, as it was called in the mid-west, to watch television.   Mr. DuBuois repacked and lit his pipe, Mrs. DuBuois picked up her crocheting.

"Hey!" Ron suddenly called out, "Where's the tree?"

Puffing softly, his dad simply said, "We was waitin' on you to get home to buy it.   You and I always pick out our tree together.   We'll get it tomorrow."

Without dropping a stitch, his mom added, "We'll string popcorn and cranberries, too."

Settling back on the old, comfortable couch next to Julie, Ron told her, "This is why I wanted so much to be here for the holidays, so much tradition."

She nodded and took his hand in hers.

Wednesday morning broke cold and bleak in Dayton.   Detective Ogsten and Chief Myers had been behind closed doors most of the morning with F.B.I. Agent Ken Gillis, filling him in on what they knew and what they surmised.   Gillis listened, and took notes.

He was not at all familiar with the case here in Ohio, nor the others in Denver or Chicago. "What else did you get from Chicago? Their information seemed a little sketchy."

"Nothing more than we told you. We're waiting for more to come through."

Standing and putting away his pad and pen, Gillis informed the anxious officers that there was little the bureau could, or would be able to do until there was a positive I.D. on the suspect and they had issued a warrant for his arrest. "When you get that, call us." He nodded as he left, "Gentlemen."

Neither Ogsten nor Myers spoke for a long time. Finally, Ogsten broke the silence. "What now?"

"I don't know." Myers sighed, "We can't wait long, New Year's Eve is close and if Dr. Arno is right, it could be a blood bath." Myers leaned back in his chair and tented his fingers in front of his mouth, tapping his index fingers on his lips. His eyes darted back and forth, finally coming to rest on the open file in front of him. The room became thick with silence as the two men struggled to decide on their next move.

Suddenly, Myers sat up and grabbed the rolodex from his desk. His movement was so fast and unexpected that Ogsten jumped. "What?", he asked, "You got something?"

Flipping frantically through the sheets, Myers replied in a distant voice, "Maybe, just maybe. Ah! Here it is."

Ogsten walked around the Chief's desk and stared at the card. "Mark Atkinson. Who's that?"

"Hopefully," Myers said as he dialed, "Someone who can, and will help us."

The phone in the small, dreary office in Lansdale, Pennsylvania, was answered on the forth right. "Agent Atkinson. How can I help you?"

"Mark? Is that you? It's Steve, Steve Myers!"

"Steve! How the hell are you? It's been years. Where are you now?"

"Dayton."

"Dayton? What in God's name are you doing in Dayton?"

Myers laughed, "Being Chief of Police."

"No shit? That's great!" Atkinson was happy for his old friend, but hearing this news made his own situation seem all the more depressing.

Atkinson had been with the F.B.I. for over 30 years. In his early days, he'd been a top notch agent, but as laws changed in favor of the criminal, his aggressive, strong arm techniques, once admired, were now frowned upon. More often than not, he found himself on the losing side of many hard fought investigations for not following 'proper procedures'. This lack of attention to the rules resulted in the criminal being released on some technicality.

He began to butt heads with the powers in charge and found new, young agents with all their high tech equipment and sophisticated training slow to act. 'just following proper procedures' they'd tell him. 'Procedure my ass!' he'd angrily respond and walk away, frustrated.

About four years ago his growing uncooperativeness, as well as mounting complaints from other agents and his nearness to retirement caused him to be transferred to a Resident Agency, R.A. for short. R.A.'s are small, 2 to 3 men satellite offices where agents such at Atkinson are placed, and then transferred around every 5 or 6 years. The hope was that they would get frustrated enough to give up and opt for early retirement, or quit. One agent thought he'd gotten one over on the Bureau when he was sent to Puerto Rico. However, 5 years later he was transferred to Anchorage, Alaska. After one winter there, he got out.

Atkinson, however, was older, had more years in and was closer to retirement. He was determined to hold on for his last 3 years and retire with full pension and benefits. 'Besides,' he told his wife, 'Life here in Lansdale isn't all that bad.'

After a few minutes of idle conversation, Myers got to the real reason for his call, "Mark, I need a favor."

"What is it?"

Myers gave him all the information they'd acquired, then asked his favor. "Since we don't have a positive identity on this guy, the Bureau can't get involved, but I was hoping that maybe you could do a little investigating for us. Off the record, of course."

"Oh, of course, What exactly do you want me to do?"

"Well, we know he's been moving east. We've got a good description, his aliases, and a decent composite. If I fax this to you I was hoping you'd be able to work your special charm with the local police and sheriff departments, find out if he's been seen or better yet, if anyone knows who the hell he really is!"

Nodding, Atkinson agreed. "I can do that. After all, I'm still as charming as ever!" He laughed at his own joke, Myers smiled, unseen by Atkinson.

"There is one more detail, and if this puts you off I'll understand."

"What is it?" I've probably had experience with it already." Now Myers laughed.

"I doubt it. The guy we're looking for is gay."

Myers waited for a response. Finally, after a long pause, it came.

"Oh! Well that I haven't had any experience with, professionally or personally. But, hey, he's killing people, right? So I don't care that he's gay, he's just another low life to me."

"Good, Then I can count on you?"

"Sure you can. I don't know how much help I'll be, but send me what you have and I'll spread the word around. One place I know I'll get help from is the State Police."

"How so?"

"Through their Gay Officers League."

"Oh, yeah, that's right. Glad you thought about that. I'd completely forgotten."

"Well, not many people, even in law enforcement, are aware of that organization. And if this guy is offing other gay men, I'm sure they'll be a big help."

"Mark, I don't know how to thank you."

"Don't thank me yet. I haven't done anything."

"Just trying is a big help to us, believe me. I'll get the information out to you today."

"Good, I'll be in touch as soon as I get anything."

They spoke for a short while longer then hung up.

"What do you think?" Ogsten asked.

"I'm not thinking, Sam. I'm praying."

Chapter 10 — DECEMBER 27th

Ron wanted this time to pass in slow motion, but, as usual, it flew by. Before he knew it, he was saying good-bye to his family at the train station. Julie helped him carry the extra bags with gifts, and of course, food, onto the train.

Making sure her parents were out of sight, Julie pulled a folded paper from her coat pocket. "Ronnie, listen. I didn't want to say anything in front of mom and dad, but,..." she hesitated, "Here, take this and please be careful."

"Jules, what are you babbling about?" He opened the paper as Julie continued in a hushed voice. Pointing to the composite, she told Ron, "This guy has already killed at least 3 men, one right here in Chicago. There could have been others, the police aren't sure. They think he may be heading east. So far, the victims have only been older men, but you never know. And, they've all been committed around holidays. New Year's Eve is right around the corner. For God's sake, be careful and tell all your friends to do the same."

He looked at Julie and saw the concern in her eyes, "I promise you I won't look at a man until he's caught. Besides, we're heading to the peace and quiet of the Poconos. This," he pointed to the composite, "Says he's heading to a major city, like New York or Boston."

"Ronnie!" Julie was upset at her brother's casual attitude towards this.

Throwing up his hands in surrender, he gave in. "Okay, I swear I'll be careful."

"Good." Julie gave him a kiss good-bye and left the train.

Ron studied the drawing and reread the description, and the aliases he'd used. 'He looks familiar.' Ron thought as he folded the composite and tucked it into his coat pocket. He studied the drawing several times on the long train ride back to Philadelphia, asking himself why this guy looked so familiar, hoping to spark some memory, but nothing came to him. He dropped it on the empty seat beside him and stared out the dreary, winter landscape.

Ron found himself smiling, despite the overcast weather. Being home for Christmas had been a tonic for him. He loved his work, enjoyed the excitement, the attention of the audience, as well as the company of his fellow entertainers, but unlike the others in the group, he kept close to his family, calling frequently, writing and sending postcards and small gifts from cities they performed in. He longed for that kind of life, a home, one person to love, Sunday dinners and holidays spent with family and friends. He knew one day he'd meet a man who shared these values, maybe Anthony, he didn't know. He kept trying in every city they performed in, looking into the audience for a face that said, 'Here I am.' So far nothing. The longer it went on, the more defeated he became.

As the Amtrack Express sped past cities and farms, his thoughts drifted back to a talk he'd had with Anthony on the drive back to Harold's apartment after their Cartwheel engagement. Ron was sitting in the back of the van, quiet and withdrawn. Noticing this, Anthony came back and asked, "Hey, what's wrong? You're not yourself."

Smiling sadly he took Anthony's hand, "Just a little tired I guess. All this traveling we've been doing lately is starting to get to me."

"Liar. It's more than that and you know it." Sliding into the bench seat next to him, Anthony continued, "You need to talk about anything? You know I'm a good listener."

"No, not yet, anyway. Maybe later. Could you just sit with me for a while?"

"Of course." Anthony put his arm around Ron. It felt so good. They sat quietly for a while.

"Anthony, do you ever regret your decision to stay with the group? I mean wouldn't you rather have a home, a lover, and all that other stuff?"

"So that's what this is all about?" Anthony sat up a bit, removed his arm from around Ron and took both his hands. "Honey, you've got a long time to find your mate and settle down. The worst thing you can do is try to force it, especially when you're the entertainment at a resort or a club. It isn't going to happen there.

"I've seen the way you look at men in the audience. Don't do that to yourself. He's not going to show up one night in a tux, carrying a dozen red roses, and take you away from all this. That, if you'll pardon the pun, is the stuff of fairy tales.

"You'll meet him when you least expect it. Maybe in a super market, a restaurant, or even walking down the street at home. A friend of mine met his lover in P-Town just that way, walking down the street. It was instantaneous, he told me, a look, a smile, and 'click' it happened. They've been together almost 8 years now."

Ron sighed, "I'm beginning to think he's passed by me already and I was too busy to notice him. I'm lonely, Anthony. Don't you ever get lonely?"

"Of course I do, and it doesn't help when I'm on stage and I see couples holding hands, exchanging a secret laugh, or a quick kiss."

They sat in silence for a while longer, Ron staring blankly ahead. Anthony pulled him close, "I want to tell you one story, then I'll shut up. Years ago, I guess it was either '94, or '95, just after Jim, my first lover, and I broke up. I went out to California for vacation to visit friends, Andy and Tom. I had a wonderful time until the night we went to a play. There were 7 or 8 of us, all men, dressed in suits, looking good. After the play we went to one guy's house for a small party. Those guys were all so gorgeous, and seemed so happy. I started getting depressed thinking about the break up. I didn't realize it at the time, but I physically pulled away from the group, got wrapped up in my own thoughts. I went through the motions of conversation, but I wasn't really there.

"The next morning, I was in the backyard, playing with their Golden Retriever when Andy came out. 'What's wrong with you?' he asked. 'Nothing. I'm fine.' I told him. He took me by the hand and led me to a bench in the corner of the yard. 'I've known you for a long time, don't tell me nothing is wrong.' I couldn't reply, he was right. 'I know you're thinking about Jim and what happened, but you're ruining your own good time and affecting others around you.' I didn't think anyone even noticed me, or thought my behavior was out of the ordinary. 'Last night,' he continued, 'a few of those guys approached me about you. They thought you were so good looking, some of them wanted to ask you out, or to go home with them, but they were afraid to approach you, you looked so distant.'

"I was shocked, I didn't think any of those guys even looked at me. Then he told me something so simple, but so profound, I never forgot it. He said, 'Your problems are going to be home when you get there, deal with them then. For now, be where you are.'

"That one statement had such an impact on me. It was the best advice I've ever gotten." He looked at Ron and saw his lips mimic the phrase, then a smile appeared.

"I think I get it." Ron said, "I'm missing out on the here and now worrying about what might or might not come to be. How simple!" He sat up and hugged Anthony. "Thank you. Your friend is genius, and so are you for knowing when to share his wisdom."

Returning the embrace, Anthony simply said, "Hey, what are friends for? Come on, we'd better get back up to the front of the van before the rest of the group starts thinking we're back here having wild sex!"

They got up and started walking forward, Ron watching Anthony's butt the whole way. 'Not a bad idea.' he thought.

Chapter 11 — DECEMBER 28th

Although the first guests were still hours from arriving, Jonathan was already hard at work. He walked through each room in the main lodge, checking each for fresh sheets, towels, toiletries, and general cleanliness. He had to laugh to himself as he did this. The rooms were small and contained furniture right out of the 40's and 50's, right down to the chenille bed spreads, left here when the lodge was new. Satisfied that they were well prepared, he next checked the lobby. Since this room was the first one guests would see, he wanted it to be as nearly perfect as possible. After a careful inspection, he was satisfied. It looked comfortable and inviting. Groupings of overstuffed, leather arm chairs were clustered about the large room, for guests to relax and talk in. An antique, claw leg table and chairs sat in the far left corner, behind it stood an old bookcase, stacked with board games, everything from Monopoly to Trivial Pursuit, to be enjoyed by guests. Magazines of interest to the gay community were arranged on the several dark pine occasional tables near the chairs. The piano was on the right hand side of the room, near the dining room, tuned and ready to be played and enjoyed.

The small gift shop, next to the registration desk along the back wall of the lobby, was fully stocked with T-shirts, key chains, and other gifts with the Lambda Lodge insignia. There were also rainbow flag decals for car windows as well as earrings, ties, and even cuff-links with the rainbow motif. The fresh cut holiday tree was still perfuming the room with the scent of balsam, and the multi-colored lights twinkled and reflected off of the glass ornaments, many of which had been gifts of former guests. It was a warm, cozy room, and Jonathan smiled as he pulled on his coat to make sure both the Rainbow House and Mt. Nebo House met his approval.

The police composites had arrived about 10 days ago, and Jonathan made a point of posting them in the lobby, dining room and disco. He'd also hand delivered some to each gay and lesbian bar in town, stressing the importance of posting them in highly visible places. Everyone was more than glad to help, but questioned the likelihood of this guy showing up in the Poconos. "Look," Jonathan told them, "He could show up anywhere, and besides, what if someone from here is going to one of these cities for New Year's Eve, you'd want them to return safely, wouldn't you? And not become the next victim." Some hadn't even considered that possibility.

His father had called again, informing Jonathan of the discovery of a third victim, as well as the use of the letter 'z' in the last name. This information, as well as the name and phone number of Agent Atkinson, was added to the bottom of the composite. Jonathan hoped it would never have to be used.

At Lambda Lodge and Resort, Charlie had already checked and rechecked the guests' registrations. No one with the last name beginning with a 'z' had reserved a room, or was on the waiting list, now defunct, since there had been no cancellations. When Charlie had asked Jonathan why he wanted the waiting list checked, he was surprised, "Charlie, if he's on it, my dad and the other police departments working on these crimes could have a much needed lead."

Jonathan returned to the lodge after checking the out buildings. They needed a little more work, ice was forming on the porch steps to the Rainbow House and in the parking lot of Mt. Nebo House, he instructed the grounds crew to get right on it.

Tim, working the front desk, looked up and smiled as Jonathan entered, "Hi", boss!" Tim was just shy of his 30th birthday, blonde and quite attractive. He was very personable and all the guests liked him. Many of the single men who vacationed at the resort had asked him out, but he refused, saying that he didn't like to get involved with guests, even though he was very tempted at times. He did, however, develop a very deep liking for one man who visited several times a year and was registered for this New Year's Eve. Tim was looking forward to seeing him again.

"Hi." Jonathan responded, stamping snow off of his shoes and hanging up his coat, scarf, and gloves. "Anyone check in yet?"

"Nah. It's still early. A few people are due later this afternoon, but the big rush won't be until tomorrow. Stacy is coming in early to help with the check in."

"Good. What about NuView. Are they here yet?"

"Harold did call," he picked up the stack of messages that had come in that day. "Let's see. Ah!

Here it is. He said they'd be here later this afternoon, barring any unforeseen problems. Their rooms are ready, so you can relax."

"I hope I can. Have you seen Charlie?"

Tim pointed, "In the kitchen," and turned his attention to the ringing phone. When he hung up he looked through the list of reservations again to find out which room Gary Adams, the man he liked, would be staying in. To his delight, Gary was staying in the lodge, a single. Tim couldn't understand why a man like Gary was still single. He was attractive, intelligent and a genuinely nice person. Last year he'd spent most of his time in the lobby alone, writing. He'd had several poems and short stories published and was working on his first novel. When it was published later that year, Tim received an autographed copy. Gary had signed it, 'To a young man who holds a special place in my heart.'

Tim was delighted when he read that, and showed it to everyone, guests as well as staff. He read the book in a few days and thoroughly enjoyed it. He made a point of sending a thank you card to

Gary, and was sure to mention that he was looking forward to seeing him soon. Now he couldn't wait to see him walk through the front door. As he stared at the reservation card, he wondered if he could really be falling for this man. Despite their age difference there was a connection between them, something he couldn't quite put his finger on. It was a sense, a feeling he got when he thought of Gary. Maybe this time he'd be willing to break his own rule and spend some of his off time with Gary.

Jonathan and Charlie came out of the dining room, talking in whispers. Charlie looked up in time to see Tim hastily put the reservation cards away. He nudged Jonathan, who looked up to see a red-faced Tim behind the desk, his hands casually clasped behind his back.

"So, Tim," Charlie started the teasing, "Problems with a reservation?"

"No, no. Everything's fine. Just checking the, ah, the room assignments."

"Oh," Jonathan joined in, "And what room is Gary in?"

As his bosses leaned on the desk, smirking, Tim gave in. "Okay, you caught me. I'm sorry, but I really like this guy. He's one of the most genuine, affectionate men I've ever met. Not to mention good-looking and hot!"

"So, what's the problem?" Charlie asked. "You like him and we know he's fond of you. Go for it!"

Tim was a little taken aback, "Really? You wouldn't mind?"

Confused, Jonathan asked, "Why would we mind?"

"Well, I mean, he's a guest, and you know how I feel about that. I don't know, it wouldn't be right. Would it?"

Shaking his head, Jonathan put Tim's fears aside, "Sweetheart, you're a terrific young man. Both of us want you to find someone. So what if he's a guest. That's your silly rule, not ours. If what you're feeling is real, don't let anything stand in your way, not even yourself."

Tim looked back and forth between his bosses, then smiled. "I'll do it. I'll ask him out."

Jonathan and Charlie both kissed him on the cheek. "Good," Jonathan said. "It's about time!" replied Charlie. They left for their rooms to rest up for what was going to be a non-stop 3 day party. Tim started thinking of the best time and the best way to ask Gary out. Time started passing too slowly for him, he was anxious now.

Ron couldn't shake the bad feeling that came over him on the way to Lambda Lodge. It was a gnawing sensation in the pit of his stomach that he couldn't attribute to any one cause. He tried remembering Anthony's advice, 'be where you are', it helped a little, but the ominous feeling stayed with him and grew stronger as they drew nearer to the Poconos. He kept the feeling to himself, knowing the others in the group wouldn't take him seriously, and as long as he was occupied he thought he'd be okay.

They arrived at Lambda Lodge at dusk, about 4:30 this time of year. The sky was gray and low, heavy with snow. Maybe that's what was eating at him, getting snowed in here, away from home, losing power, the feeling of being trapped. He just didn't know.

His first glimpse of the lodge was both reassuring and foreboding. The quiet beauty of the main building, comfortably nestled in the mountains was the picture of serenity, but at the same time, the dark, barren trees, standing in stark contrast to the luminescent, blue-white snow was disconcerting, right out of a B horror movie. He half expected to see a chainsaw wielding psychopath emerge from the dark woods. He had to laugh at this unfounded fear as they started unloading the van.

Charlie and Jonathan greeted them and took them to their rooms, a small house actually, just behind the lodge. The house was cozy, a large combination kitchen and living room and 2 bedrooms. The couch in the living room opened into a full size bed, 'quite comfortable', Charlie assured them. The kitchen had been stocked with food, drinks and snacks. Everyone seemed pleased.

Charlie and Jonathan left them to get settled in, telling them that dinner was at 7:00.

As they scrambled back and forth to the van, unpacking, Ron felt his heart race. The gnawing feeling in his stomach was turning to pure fear. He knew something was wrong here. He stopped Anthony as they unloaded, "Can I ask you a favor?" he asked, his voice trembling slightly.

"Sure. What is it?" Anthony asked, grabbing the final few bags from the van.

"Will you stay with me? I mean, share a room?"

Anthony was flattered, "I'd love to!" Then noticing Ron's troubled eyes, asked, "What's wrong? You're as white as the snow."

"I'll tell you later, when we're alone. I don't want the others to hear, they'll think I'm nuts."

"Okay. Let's get this done and we can talk in the room."

The rest of the group reacted with surprise and suspicion when Anthony announced that he and Ron were going to share a room.

"See, I told you there was something going on between those two!" Steve said to Ray.

"No! It's not like that," Ron responded defensively.

"You don't have to defend yourself," Harold said, shooting Steve an angry glance, "She's just being her bitchy old self. You two take one bedroom, Steve and Ray will take the other. I'll sleep out here."

"Are you sure you'll be comfortable out here, on a pull out? We don't mind staying out here," Ray said, trying to make up from Steve's comment.

"No, I'll be fine. I probably won't even open it up. Lord knows I've fallen asleep on my own sofa at home many times. You two go on and get settled in."

Steve couldn't resist, "Yeah, just keep the noise down!" Ray slapped him, "Knock it off! Come on, let's unpack. I want to shower and rest a bit before dinner." They went to their separate rooms, leaving Harold all alone. He stood there for a minute, thinking about what Steve had said. Finally, shrugging his shoulders, and reaching for a soda from the refrigerator, he simply thought, 'Well good for them, if it's true.'

Alone in their room, the bags unpacked, Anthony stretched out on the bed, propped up on the pillows, his hands clasped behind his head. "All right, what gives? You've been pensive the whole trip up here."

"It was that obvious?" Ron asked, putting the last of his clothes in the small dresser.

Anthony nodded, "To me it was. Now come over here and tell me what's got you so worked up." He patted the bed.

Sitting on the edge of the bed, legs folded under him. Ron told Anthony about the unsettling feeling that had been working on him. It was something bad, evil even, and that it had gotten worse when they got here.

"It could just be anxiety. You're doing some new illusions this performance, you're probably afraid they won't work well."

Ron shook his head, "No, it's more than that. I've had illusions fail before, I can cover that up.

This is something more. Wait, I want to show you something." He got up and took the folded clipping from his coat pocket and handed it to Anthony. "My sister gave this to me as I left Chicago after Christmas."

As Anthony studied the drawing, and read the description, Ron continued, "She said the police think he's heading east to New York, or Boston."

Anthony returned the paper, "And...?"

Ron got up from the bed and began to pace. "And when I looked at it, I got the feeling I'd seen him before. That I could possibly know him from somewhere. And now," he stopped pacing, "Now we're here, at a popular gay resort, and we are east of Chicago."

Anthony couldn't help but laugh, "I'm sorry, Ron, but you can't seriously think he'd be coming here! Honey, this place is secluded, quiet, and somewhat expensive. I doubt a man like that would come here to murder someone! Like the police report says, he's probably in New York, or Boston by now. Don't let yourself get caught up in this unreasonable fear.

And as far as thinking you might know him, his description and the drawing could fit any of thousands of guys. You're probably confusing him with some of the people that have seen our show. You know how you cruise the audience."

Ron stood and thought for a long moment, then sat back on the bed, reaching out and rubbing Anthony's thigh. "You're right, I'm probably putting 2 and 2 together and coming up with 3 or some other ridiculous answer."

Anthony took Ron's hand in his own and pulled him up closer, "I know I'm right. Now I want you to relax." He kissed Ron's forehead, cheeks, and mouth, pulling him until their bodies were tightly pressed together. Ron responded with all the passion that had been building up inside him since the night they spent together at Woody's just before Christmas.

Eyes locked, they undressed each other, clothing carelessly tossed on the floor. Their hot hands roamed freely over each others bodies, while mouths engulfed tongues. As their breathing grew

127

heavier, their bodies pulsed together rhythmically, thrusting together harder and harder. Anthony pulled Ron on top of him, slightly opening his legs. Ron leaned up, looking into Anthony's shining, dark eyes, as he rocked his body back and forth, forcing Anthony's legs farther apart. Lowering himself between them he felt a raging desire he'd never known. As if they could read each other's thoughts. Anthony raised his knees slightly as Ron pushed forward. Then, slowly, their eyes in a fixed gaze, Ron entered him. Both men froze in that position, all motion stopped, their faces showing passion as well as disbelief. Ron looked down between their bodies, this was really happening. He looked back into Anthony's face and saw the desire he felt reflected in his eyes. Anthony grabbed Ron's head and pulled him down into a passionate kiss as their bodies pulsed and heaved against each other. Breathing became difficult as their desire grew, Ron's head nestled in the crook of Anthony's neck, as Anthony's legs wrapped ever tighter around Ron's waist, pulling him even deeper into himself, his hands reached back and kneaded Ron's butt as he thrust harder and harder.

Suddenly, Ron pushed himself up onto his palms, Anthony's one hand going to his own straining erection, "Now!" he gasped and they both released themselves, the intensity of the moment contorting both of their faces. Ron's arms trembled violently and he could no longer hold himself up. He collapsed onto Anthony, their slick bodies sliding together. They kissed over and over, passionately at first, then slower, more tenderly. They remained motionless until their breathing returned to normal, Anthony slowly lowered his legs and Ron rolled off of him. They lie cuddled together, lightly dozing for a while. Finally, Ron roused himself, "What time is it?" he asked, his voice heavy and deep.

"Who cares!" came Anthony's whispered response. As he turned on his side, Ron snuggled up to his warm body pulling him close. "You feel so good. I could lie here like this forever."

Some time later, a sharp rap on the door jolted them both, it was Harold. "It's already past 6:00. If you two want to shower before going to dinner you'd better hurry." They'd both forgotten about anyone else being in the house and possibly hearing them.

Harold continued, "Steve and Ray are already at the lodge, have been for about an hour." Both Ron and Anthony breathed a sigh of relief. "And," came Harold's voice from behind the closed door again, "I didn't hear a thing!"

When they finally arrived at the lodge, an hour later, Harold apologized for them, "We got to talking and time just flew by!" He didn't want Steve starting up again, he didn't. Conversation over dinner centered on the lodge, how wonderfully cozy it was, how superb for food was. "Are all the meals like this?" Ray asked. Receiving an affirmative reply, he quipped, "Well, there goes the diet." Not that he needed one, Ray was always thin.

Sometime during the meal, Ron noticed the same drawing his sister had given him hanging in the dining room. Nudging Anthony, he whispered, "Look!" motioning to the wall near the door. They both stopped eating and looked at each other in surprise.

Jonathan, who had been standing at the matre de's podium, noticed this and turned to see what had distracted them. Realizing it was one of the composites his father had sent, he approached their table.

Ron didn't wait for any greeting or small talk when he saw Jonathan approaching. "What do you know about him?" he asked, pointing to the sketch. Everyone now turned to look at what Ron was referring to. By now, Ron had told the group of the 3 known murders and other facts related to them, but seeing the police composite here heightened their curiosity as well as their degree of concern. They all listened intently as Jonathan told them what he knew. When he'd finished, they all began asking questions at once, many of which Jonathan couldn't answer.

Becoming aware of the noise, Charlie, who had been casually visiting guests' tables, joined the group. He somewhat quieted their fears by telling them that their guest list had been thoroughly checked, and not one z surname had been found. Also the fact that all 3 murders had been committed in major cities, not in quiet, out of the way towns such as Stoudsburg, was reassuring to everyone except Ron, it did nothing to allay his growing apprehension, and fear. Seeing the concern on his face, Anthony gently squeezed his thigh under the table, Ron took his hand and, managing a weak smile, he winked and mouthed the words, 'thank you'. This simple gesture gave Ron a great deal of comfort, and knowing they'd be sleeping together added to that feeling, as well as some arousal. He moved Anthony's hand higher and when he felt Ron's rapidly thickening erection, he choked on his meal. Grabbing his napkin to cover his mouth, Anthony apologized, "Sorry, went down the wrong pipe." and threw an amused grin at Ron.

Dinner finished, Charlie and Jonathan took the group to the disco to see the facilities. The dance floor was large and there were dressing rooms behind it, small, but adequate. The sound system was quite good, and since they did have other types of entertainment, there was good lighting. The only question was about getting dry ice for Ron's final illusion, his striptease. "That shouldn't be a problem," Charlie said as he walked to the side of the dance floor near the D.J. booth. "We have a smoke machine. We'll try that, and if it works for your illusion, we're set. If not, we can get dry ice easily."

That settled, Harold got the van and pulled it down the hill to the back of the disco and they began unloading their equipment, costumes, and props. They spent the better part of 2 hours getting things set up and put into the dressing rooms. That being done, they returned to the lodge to have a night cap before retiring.

Alone in their room again, Anthony and Ron slipped under the thick comforter, and snuggled together, gently touching and kissing. Stroking his cheek, Anthony asked, "You're still worried, aren't you?" Ron nodded. "Don't be. Jonathan's dad told him the murderer is probably in New York, or some other big city by now. He's a cop, he should know."

Pulling Anthony close, feeling the warmth of his body, Ron replied in a distant, shallow voice, "I know, but it's the 'probablies', and 'should knows' that worry me."

For the second time that day they made love and fell asleep wrapped together.

Chapter 12 — DECEMBER 29th

Antone' had packed several pairs of slacks and jeans as well as a few of his warmest sweaters, and of course, his dress boots, he hated shoes, before Richard picked him up. When Richard arrived at McNaulty's, he asked if he had a suit, or at least a sport jacket and dress slacks, shirt and tie. Seeing the embarrassment in Antone's eyes, Richard quickly said he could borrow one of his, if it fit. They returned to Richard's house, and after trying on a few suits, realized it was a futile effort. The slacks were too long, and a bit large in the waist, and the jacket sleeves hung almost to his finger tips. Rummaging through the back of this closet, Richard came across an old herringbone sports jacket in shades of camel and brown that blended well with a pair of slacks Antone' had already packed. It fit well enough, and when paired with a soft pastel blue shirt and patterned silk tie, Antone' looked great.

"You look spectacular!" Richard exclaimed, "I'll have trouble keeping the other men away from you."

Antone' put his arms around Richard's waist and pulled him close, their bodies pressing tightly together from the waist down. "They can look, but they can't touch," Antone' replied, as he rocked his hips back and forth against Richard, his hands sliding down the older man's back to fondle his firm butt, "I'm all yours."

"Let me help you out of these clothes," Richard stammered as he began undressing Antone', "We don't want to get them wrinkled."

Antone' allowed Richard to removed his jacket, tie, shirt, and unzip his slacks, which slid to the floor. He stepped out of them and started groping Richard's crotch. Richard moaned, his eyes closing, and gripped Antone' by the shoulders. Antone' unbuttoned and loosened Richard's shirt, nibbling his neck. He then unhooked and unzipped his jeans and lowered them to just below his ass. They stood there for a while exploring each other with anxious fingers, and lips, their underwear straining as they became more and more aroused. They began to sway rhythmically together, thrusting slightly, the friction of their motion sending waves of pleasure through both men as their aroused shafts rubbed and slid across each other through the thin cotton cloth. Richard began to lean towards the bed, a foot or so behind them. "No!" Antone' said sharply. Richard gazed at him, confused. Then Antone' slipped his index fingers into the elastic on Richard's briefs, and his thumbs into his own and worked both pair down, releasing them from the confining cloth. "Now, open your legs a little," Richard did, so did

Antone'. Richard gasped as Antone' took his firm erection and placed it between his own legs, then did the same to Richard with his.

"Now, close your legs." The sensation was overwhelming, they thrust and rotated their hips against each other, hands groping, squeezing and pinching, tongues licking and teeth nibbling. As they continued, sweat lubricated their hot bodies, and their movements became easier and they moved faster, the feeling of being inside each other at the same time was too much for Richard to bear, his mind short-circuiting, not able to comprehend all the sensations he felt. It wasn't long before he began moaning in a guttural voice, and exploded between Antone's thighs. Feeling this, Antone' soon joined him in trembling release. Their knees weak, and unable to keep them up, they fell back onto the bed, still locked together, bodies shaking, breathing heavy. Finally, Richard managed to speak, "My God! I've never done that before. Didn't even know it was possible."

Rolling over on his back, his chest slick with sweat, Antone' smirked, "Sure as hell beats the old missionary position, doesn't it?

"Hell yes!" Richard breathlessly replied. Leaning over he kissed Antone, "Especially with you." He got up and unsteadily walked to the bathroom to shower. Antone' began to drift off, 'Do it now,' he heard, 'Don't wait. He's more dangerous than the others.' In a groggy voice, Antone' responded, "No, not him. He's different, I like him, he's nice."

His private argument was abruptly interrupted by Richard's voice, "Paul, come in and shower with me." Glad for the chance to halt his argument with himself, Antone' joined Richard in the hot, steaming shower. 'Do it now!' he heard again.

A short time later, they packed their bags in Richard's Town Car, and started out. Antone' had told Mrs. McNautly that he was going to Philadelphia to spend the New Year with his sister and her family. She was glad to know that he would be with family, not stuck here alone on such an important holiday. She told him that she would hold all his mail, and that his room would be thoroughly cleaned upon his return, not that she ever let any of the rooms in the house get untidy. He thanked her, knowing full well that he'd never be returning to that pit. He had packed every stitch of clothing he had, and sold the rest of Walter Marqueth's jewelry a few days before. He'd already discarded the AT&T calling card and the MAC card in a street corner trash barrel. Saying good-bye to Mrs. McNaulty, and giving her a kiss for New Year, he closed the door to the house, a sense of calm descending over him, he started to believe that maybe this time he'd won the battle with the darkness.

The drive to the resort was long, but pleasant. Conversation was easy and the silent times were comfortable. As they neared the Poconos, Richard turned the radio on, "I want to hear the local weather. If there's snow we may be delayed, or detoured."

"Do you think that might happen?" Antone' asked.

Pointing eastward through the windshield, Richard said, "Those look like storm clouds, and at higher elevations, the likelihood of snow is good." Taking Antone's hand and kissing it, he cooed, "Wouldn't it be romantic if we got snowed in? I hope we have a blizzard."

Antone' hid his concern at best he could, "Yeah," He scanned the gray sky ahead, "You don't think that will happen. Do you?"

Watching the road ahead, unaware of Antone's mood change, Richard grinned, "You never know. You just never know."

Antone' remained silent, quietly fighting the voices that had started up again. 'You should have done it earlier. It would be over now. You'd be safe again.' He squeezed his eyes hard and rubbed his temples.

"Paul, are you feeling okay?" Richard asked, gently stroking his cheek. "You look worried."

"Headache, a bad one. Probably the change in the weather and the heat in the car."

Richard lowered the temperature on the climate control and cracked the windows a bit. "We can stop and get you some aspirin if you'd like."

"No, I'll be fine. I'm just going to close my eyes and rest a bit. This seat does recline, doesn't it?" Richard told him where the lever was and he reclined the seat fully. "That's good," he said, settling back and closing his eyes.

"Do you want me to turn the radio off?"

"No, but could you find a better station, or put in a CD?"

Richard slid in a Rochmananoff CD. "Better?" he asked, stroking Antone's head.

"Yes, much." Antone' kissed Richard's hand and held it to his chest.

They never heard the weather report.

Tim and Stacy were frantic at the front desk. The reports of an approaching storm brought most guests up early. By 1 P.M. all but two rooms in all three buildings were occupied.

Flopping onto one of the lobby's arm chairs, Stacy groaned, "My feet are killing me! And my back!"

"Here, let me give you a massage." Tim offered, Stacy gratefully agreed and slowly his technique relieved some of the tension and soreness in her neck and upper back. "If only you were a voluptuous blond," she crooned.

"Well, I am blond." Tim teased.

Stacy smirked, "Not good enough, I'm afraid."

The front door opened and Tim stopped his massage. "Hey!" Stacy started to protest, then looked up. It was Gary. He stood there looking more wonderful than ever, wearing an ankle length Outback coat in deep brown and carrying a monogrammed canvass bag and lap top computer. The slight scuff of a beard deepened his cheeks and accented his strong, angular face. His light hazel, or were they green, eyes peered out from his dark brows and his crooked smile rendered Tim speechless.

Tim and Stacy remained motionless. "Well, can I register?" Gary asked, breaking the silence, "And how about a hug?" He dropped his bag and placed the lap top on it, opening his arms wide as he approached Tim. "It is so good to see you!" he exclaimed as he and Tim embraced, "You look wonderful. As gorgeous as ever."

"You too." was all Tim could say as he held Gary as tightly as he dared. Fearing he would become aroused, Tim broke the embrace, but kept one arm around Gary's waist. "Come on, let's get you registered."

"Great! Hi, Stacy. How are you?" He hugged her tightly.

"I'm good," she responded with genuine affection. "God, that feels good. If only you were a woman!" she laughed as he released her.

"Sorry, Stacy. If I were a woman, I know I'd be straight. I like men too much." They laughed again, then Stacy excused herself, knowing that Tim wanted time alone with Gary.

Gary registered and took his room key. "Number 7, how lucky," he mused, winking at Tim.

Feeling flirtatious, Tim responded, "You never know, this could be a great New Year."

Smiling warmly, Gary said, "It is already. You look so good. Come here." Tim rounded the counter and was instantly embraced again, this time softer and more tenderly. "I couldn't wait to get here and see you again." As he spoke, Gary's strong hands rubbed and massaged Tim's back from top to bottom.

"Gary, don't. Not here." Tim pulled away, leaving Gary confused and a bit embarrassed.

"I'm sorry," Gary said. "I guess I was out of line. Are you seeing someone?"

Tim shook his head, "No, it's not that."

"Well, what is it then? Was I coming on too strong?"

Looking down, shrugging his shoulders, Tim mumbled, "A little, I guess." He walked over and sat in one of the leather covered arm chairs near the tree. Gary followed and sat on the sofa, opposite him. Tim unconsciously picked at the tree, glancing at Gary, not knowing how to start.

Moving to the edge of the sofa, Gary implored, "Talk to me, Tim. Tell me what's on your mind, please."

Tim tentatively started, "I don't know how to start, or even what to say. I feel so stupid. How could I have even thought..." He paused, took a deep breath, and looking Gary straight in the eye started again, "Okay, it's no secret that I'm very attracted to you."

Gary nodded, "I know that. And..."

Tim help up a hand, stopping him from completing his thought. "I think the feeling is mutual. Am I right?"

Sitting back again, Gary agreed, "You know I'm very fond of you, have been for a while."

Tim got up and turned away, facing the tree. Gary came up beside him and in a voice just above a whisper, asked, "Tim, where are you going with this?"

Without looking at him, Tim let himself say aloud what has been in his head all these months, "I guess I'm afraid. I mean, sure there's an attraction, but there are so many differences. You're a writer, you're educated, and worldly. I'm a desk clerk for a small gay resort. I never finished college, and my only world has been the Poconos, and the Jersey shore. Besides," he began picking at the tree again, "I'm so much younger than you. I feel so, so..."

Grabbing him by the shoulders, and facing him, Gary put a quick stop to where he thought Tim was going with this. "Don't you dare say you feel immature, or stupid, or anything remotely like that! You're none of those things. Tim, look at me," he picked Tim's head up so that their eyes were mere inches apart. "First of all, you run this lodge. I know, Jonathan and Charlie own the place, but it's you who runs the day to day business, isn't it?" Tim shrugged. "And where did you get the idea that I was so worldly? I don't travel much at all, most of the time it's for book signings, not for pleasure. Most of what you call my 'worldliness' comes from doing research for my novels and the many nights I spend alone at home watching the History Channel, or the Learning Channel. As for our age difference, I don't give a damn, plain and simple. If something works for two people, it works. End of story."

Tim timidly looked into Gary's eyes, they were green, "You really mean that, don't you?"

"I certainly do." Laughing a bit to himself, Gary moved his hands to cup Tim's face, "Truth be known, I thought I was way too old for you."

Eyes widening, Tim exclaimed, "No, not at all! I mean you're not old at all. Not to me."

Returning to the sofa, Gary asked Tim if there was anything else on his mind. His confidence boosted, Tim sat next to Gary, who immediately pulled him close. Looking softly into his eyes, Tim asked, "Would you spend this holiday time with me? Go out, get to know each other on a personal level and see what happens?"

Reaching up with his free hand, Gary pulled Tim close and kissed him softly, "I'd love to," he whispered.

Leaning back on the sofa, cuddled in Gary's arms, Tim exhaled deeply.

"Feeling better?"

"Much," Tim answered and reached up to give Gary another, longer kiss. Outside the snow had begun to fall.

The opening of the font door rudely ended the warm, romantic moment Gary and Tim were sharing. Tim grudgingly returned to the front desk to welcome the next, and the last, guests, and have them register. It was then that he heard whispering and laughter coming from behind the dining room door, adjacent to the lobby. "Oh great," he thought, as he greeted the couple, "Now everyone will know! Ah, who cares, for once I'm happy."

"It's started already?" Tim asked, noticing the snow on the new arrivals' coats.

"Boy has it! Was this in the forecast?" asked Richard as he shook the snow out of his hair.

"Afraid so. At least 8 inches with another storm front right behind it. Your name?"

"Pauley. Richard Pauley. We're in the lodge."

"Here it is. If you'd complete the card with the type of car and plate number, I'll get your key." Turning to pick up the key to room 6, he added, "Your guest can sign at the bottom, where indicated."

As Tim handed the key to Richard, he noticed some commotion in the dining room out of the corner of his eye, and started laughing. Confused by this behavior, Richard asked if there was something wrong with the registration card.

"Oh, no. I'm sorry. I think I'm going to have to strangle our lesbian chef!" he said loud enough for Lauren to hear. Glancing in the direction of the dining room, Richard saw a flash of white disappear into the kitchen through the swinging door. "Just as long as you don't do it before she prepares New Year's dinner."

"I won't, promise," Tim said as he filed the card without looking at it. "She and a few others have been spying on me and my man. Room 6 is at the top of the stairs in the front, on the left. Enjoy your stay."

Richard thanked Tim and he and Antone' picked up their bags. Passing Gary, who hadn't moved from the sofa, Richard nodded in greeting, Antone', however, simply stared. 'Another one,' he heard. 'They're all over and all alike. You have to stop him as well. Save that other young man as well as yourself.' He snapped back as Richard called to him, "Come on Paul. Let's unpack and get dinner, I'm starved."

Returning to the sofa, and the warmth of Gary's arms, Tim playfully said, "Well, they were the last guests, so I'm all yours. Think you can handle it?"

"I can, and then some. What did you have in mind?"

Tim looked out the picture window, then pulled Gary up. "Let's go for a walk."

"You're on. Then some hot chocolate to warm us up."

They got into their coats and slipped on their gloves. As they headed out, Tim couldn't resist telling Gary, "Honey, with what I have in mind, you won't need hot chocolate to warm you up."

They ran into the swirling snow, hurling handfuls at each other, laughing like school boys on holiday.

Antone' watched them from behind the curtain in room 6, his eyes wide, and his breathing shallow. He stared at them until they faded into the darkness of the night. 'Save him' he heard again. 'Save yourself.' Dropping the curtain, and turning to watch Richard get ready for dinner, he silently replied, 'I can't, you can't make me do it.'

As Antone' fought the darkness, his breathing returned to normal. He was in control again, but for how long? Could he ever win this battle? He could feel the darkness creeping in on him.

PART II

THE STORM

Chapter 13 — DECEMBER 30th

Up to 6 inches of fresh snow blanketed the streets of Pittsburgh. As Millie carefully picked her way through the snow on Penn Avenue to De Luca's Cafe, she pulled her collar tightly around her neck to guard against the blowing snow. There was little she could do, though, to keep the slush from sliding into her boots and chilling her feet. She winced as the cold dampness chilled her toes, but had to marvel at the deep quiet in the city, "This is nice. Cold, but nice." Not having to watch too carefully for traffic because of the snow and the holidays, she was able to walk most of the way in the street, which was much clearer than the yet unshoveled sidewalk. She was grateful when she finally got into the warm diner.

"Mornin', Al," she called to the owner and chief short order cook, Al Nicklous.

"Morning," he called back, not bothering to look up from the griddle where eggs were frying for the few customers who'd ventured out this early in the snow. "Grab yourself a cup of coffee and warm up. I've got all the orders goin'."

"Thanks." Millie poured a mug of hot coffee for herself and took a stool at the far end of the counter. Holding the steaming mug in both hands to warm them, she glanced at the newspaper Al brought in each morning. The lead story was, of course, the weather and the usual problems associated with it; power outages, poor road conditions as well as the possibility of more of the same tomorrow. "Is this ever going to end?" she remarked.

"Yeah, by spring!"

Millie giggled as she turned pages, scanning the after Christmas sale ads. Her attention was caught by a sketch with the caption, 'SUSPECT IN KILLING SOUGHT' she looked at the drawing then froze. "My God!" her voice trembled. She stared at the picture, trying to convince herself that she was mistaken, but she knew she wasn't. She quickly skimmed the article, 'Wanted for questioning in murders in Denver, Chicago, and Dayton. Believed to be headed east toward New York.'

There was a special 800 number for information leading to his arrest. Millie grabbed her check pad and a pen, wrote the number down and shoved it into her apron pocket. Although still chilled, she broke out into a sweat. 'It couldn't be, he was such a nice young man. I must be mistaken.' She picked up the mug from the counter, noticing her hand was shaking.

"Millie!"

"Oh, Al, sorry."

"You okay? You look pale."

Wiping her brow, she shook her head, "I'm fine. Orders up?"

"Yeah, table 2."

She flashed him a quick smile and picked up the plates.

The day was slow and she couldn't shake the horrible feeling that kept growing in her as the day dragged on. By mid afternoon, the diner was empty. Al decided to close early, saying that it was costing more to stay open. Millie agreed, and started cleaning up, anxious to make the call she was dreading. Locking the door, Al asked her if she wanted a lift home.

"Ah, no, that's okay. I'm not going right home. Friends live right around the corner on Spring Street, and I'm gonna' stop in and spend some time with them. Thanks anyway."

"Be careful walking, and Happy New Year, Mil," he kissed her on the cheek.

"You too. See you on Sunday." She started off as quickly as she dared towards McNaulty's.

Adelle McNaulty was shocked to see Millie standing at her door, especially considering the weather. "What on earth are you doing here?"

Pushing past her, trying to catch her breath, Millie asked, "Do you have today's paper?"

"Yes, it's in the living room. Why?"

"Get it."

"What ever for?"

"Adelle, just get the damn paper!"

Stunned by Millie's insistent behavior, and language, Adelle backed away, somewhat concerned. A few moments later she returned, the paper still in its plastic jacket.

Millie snatched the paper away and started ripping through the pages. Finding what she was looking for, she folded it over, "Look," she held the paper out in front of Adelle, "Does he look familiar?"

Adelle put on her glasses and took the paper. In a moment she slowly lowered it and stared in shock at Millie. "It's the... Oh, it can't be!" She looked at it again. "It does resemble him. Millie, what do we do?"

Millie searched her pockets, then grabbed the paper from Adelle. "Here!" she said, pointing to the 800 number, "We call this number."

Eyes wide, Adelle drew back, "You can't be serious! What if we're wrong? Why right now he's in Philadelphia preparing to celebrate the holiday with his sister."

Millie's mouth dropped, "Where's the phone?" Adelle pointed.

Millie dialed the number as quickly as she could move her arthritic fingers. It felt like forever before someone answered. "Dayton Police Department, Officer Lopez speaking."

Millie was surprised when she heard Dayton. Thinking she misdialed, she asked if this was the correct number for information on the murder suspect.

"Yes, ma'am. Do you have information for us?"

"I, I'm not sure, I could be wrong, but I think he was here, in Pittsburgh."

Grabbing a pen and pad, Lopez asked for her name, address, and phone number. Millie hesitated.

"Ma'am? Are you still there?"

"Yes, I'm here. Why do you need that information from me?"

"In case we need to contact you, depending on the information you give us. We have no leads and only a few clues to go on. Anything you tell us would be of great help."

"Well, in that case. But I don't have much to tell you." Millie gave Officer Lopez the personal information he requested then told him all she could, including the possibility of him heading for Philadelphia for the New Year. Officer Lopez took down every piece of information, then before hanging up, double checked the phone number she'd given him, she verified it then added Adelle's to it.

"Oh Millie. I hope that was the right thing to do." Adelle had listened nervously, silently hoping that nothing would come from the call. "I hope that phone never rings again."

Her hand still on the cradled receiver, Millie shook her head. "Adelle, I don't know what's going to happen." Neither could speak for a long time.

Officer Lopez immediately took the information to Chief Myers. "Finally something new to go on!" he exclaimed as he scanned the page. Most of the facts were all too familiar; a young, attractive man, new in town, and his surname started with a Z. There were gaps, however. There was no mention of him meeting or spending time with an older man, nor was there anything to make Myers think he wasn't just visiting his sister, and would return to Pittsburgh after the holiday. Other questions arose in the Chief's mind as well. Did he have a car? If so what make, model, year? Did he use it to go to his sister's, or did he take a bus, or train?

Chief Myers picked up the phone and dialed the number Millie had left. Getting no answer, he dialed the second number.

"Hello."

"This is Chief Myers, Dayton Police Department calling. Is this Mildred Fergueson?"

Adelle cupped the phone, "Millie!," she whispered, "It's the police chief from Dayton, he wants to talk to you."

Millie got up from the table in the McNaulty's small kitchen, where she and Adelle had been having tea, and took the phone. She was much calmer now, her mind cleared of the confusion of earlier in the day. "This is Millie."

"Ms. Fergueson, this is Chief Myers, Dayton P.D. Do you have a few minutes to answer some questions?"

"Yes Chief. Please call me Millie."

"Alright. Millie, some of what you told Officer Lopez was familiar to us, although you did add to our knowledge of this man. My questions deal more with what you didn't tell the officer."

"I don't think I understand, Chief."

"For example, did he have a car?"

"No, I don't think so. I believe he said he'd taken a bus into town."

"Do you know if he'd made any friends since he arrived?"

"I don't know. Could you hold on?" She held the receiver to her chest, "Adelle, did he make any friends that you know of?"

Adelle thought for a moment, "Why yes. He did spend quite of bit of time with one man."

Millie relayed the information.

"Do you know his name?"

Millie, frustrated by having to relay the questions and answers, shoved the phone into Adelle's hand, over her protests. Confused by the commotion on the other end of the line, Chief Myers called into the receiver. When someone finally answered, he knew it wasn't Millie. "Who is this?"

"This is Adelle McNaulty. I own the house where Mr. Zimza rented a room."

"I see. Ms. McNaulty, Millie said that Mr. Zimza had been spending some time with a certain man since he arrived in Pittsburgh. Do you know who that might be?"

"I'm sorry, I don't."

"Well can you tell me what he looked like?"

As Adelle thought, she bit her lower lip. Shaking her head, she told Chief Myers that the only thing she remembered was that he was somewhat older, maybe in his late 50's. "I thought he might be a relative."

"The report I have says that he went to Philadelphia to celebrate the New Year with his sister. When did he leave?"

"Yesterday, late morning."

"Did he go by car?"

"Yes, he did. The older gentlemen he knew picked him up."

"Did you notice what kind of car he was driving?"

"No, I didn't. I do remember that it was a big car. A Cadillac, or Lincoln, I think."

"One more thing," Chief Myers was hoping against hope that the answer to his next question would be yes, "Did he happen to leave his sister's name, or maybe a phone number where he could be reached?"

"No nothing like that. I didn't even think to ask."

Frustrated by not having a direct lead, but glad to know at least where he could be, Chief Myers thanked Adelle and told her that he might be in touch with her again, Millie too. Before he hung up he told her to call any time of day or night if they thought of anything else that could help, he also wished them a Happy New Year.

Adelle slowly hung up. Staring at the phone she absently said, "I never, in my wildest dreams, thought I'd ever be talking to a police officer about someone who is living in my house being involved in a crime. A murder no less!"

Millie came to her, "Adelle, we had to."

Chief Myers immediately got things rolling. He contacted Dan Winslow, head of homicide in Pittsburgh, informing him that the suspected serial killer they have been hunting for in Ohio had been sighted in his city. He gave Winslow the address and phone number of McNaulty's. "Dan, get a search warrant quick! With any luck there will be some viable prints or some other usable evidence still in his room."

Winslow set the wheels in motion, and before long had the necessary document in hand. He also made sure that another sweep of the gay bars in the city was conducted to see if anyone knew the man Zimza had allegedly left town with. The police in Philadelphia were contacted. They instituted their own resweep of the many gay bars in the city. Since it was thought that Zimza was headed there, all surrounding communities with a sizable gay population were notified of this latest information. Police in these areas redoubled their efforts to heighten awareness among gay men, especially older men. Meanwhile, the search of Zimza's room at McNaulty's yielded no new forensic evidence. Adelle had kept her promise to him and had thoroughly cleaned the room.

Hoping that this new evidence as to Zimza's whereabouts would result in a quick arrest, Chief Myers took a few moments to relax and think. Suddenly he remembered one other thing he had to do.   Flipping through the rolodex, he grabbed the phone one more time and quickly dialed.

"Agent Atkinson."

"Mark, Steve Myers here.   I've got some information for you."

"Good, I haven't been able to scare up the littlest bit of anything around here.   Nobody's aware of anything. What do you have?"

"I just got off the phone with a woman in Pittsburgh.   She said the guy we're looking for is either headed for or already in Philly. He's using a new alias, too. Paul Zimza."

"Got it, anything else?"

"Yeah, he's traveling with an older man, probably his next victim.   They left Pittsburgh yesterday morning, driving either a Cadillac, or Lincoln. That's about all I can tell you."

"Well, it's not much, but it's more than I had. I'll pass along this new information to the locals."

"Philly has already been notified, Dan Winslow took care of that for me."

"Good, that makes it easier. There aren't too many other places in the area that would attract a large gay crowd. One thing I am going to do is contact G.O.A.L. ."

"Good. We need all the help we can get. Tomorrow is New Year's Eve, and I don't want another murder being committed. Call me if you get anything."

"I will. Happy New Year, Steve."

"Yeah you too."

Chapter 14 – DECEMBER 31st

Morning on Mt. Nebo broke bright and clear, the latest front having dumped another 7 inches of new snow before moving out. Having always been an early riser, Antone' slipped out of bed and was showered and dressed before 8:00. The dining room was still closed, but he heard noise in the kitchen. Peeking in, he saw the kitchen staff busily prepping food for breakfast, and asked if he could get a cup of coffee. Tina poured him a mug full and after thanking her went out onto the porch. The silence was deafening, and the views of the surrounding mountains were breathtakingly beautiful. The snow following the slopes and rises, changing in color from stark white in the direct sun, to a glistening blue under the shadow of the towering pines. It was then he noticed the cabins, tucked into the rising mountainside. They looked deserted, and cold. Strange, he thought, to have them here, but not occupied. He wanted to look around, walk up the hill past the cabins, but the snow was far too deep, he'd have to just look for now. Later, after the roads had been plowed and the walks shoveled, he'd walk around, hopefully alone, he wanted some time to be by himself. He'd been with Richard almost every minute for the past 36 hours, and was beginning to feel caged, even though he found himself enjoying Richard's company.

He heard an engine and looked up to see a plow coming down the winding road. Next he heard a snow blower, a lodge employee was beginning to clear the paths to the various buildings. Now that it was getting noisy, he returned to the lobby. A few guests were there, waiting for the dining room to open. They cheerfully greeted him then went back to reading, or conversation. Tim wasn't behind the desk, 'probably with that man,' he heard. It was then he saw the poster, the police composite, and froze. The drawing was rough, but resembled him a great deal. He had to get rid of it. Scanning the lobby once more, making sure no one was watching him, he casually walked over to the counter, pretending to be looking at the various gift items in the display case. He then moved over to the wall near the dining room where a bulletin board advertised many of the local sights. Ever so slowly he raised his left arm and leaned on the wall, his hand coming to rest directly on the composite. As he 'read', he carefully pulled the sketch from the board and, pushing himself away, crumpled the paper and stuck it in his coat pocket. He'd have to be vigilant, there could be more of these scattered throughout the lodge and its other buildings.

The doors to the dining room opened and the guests who were seated or milling about the lobby went in for breakfast, Antone' waited. Tina asked if he wanted a table, he declined, "I'm waiting for someone, but I could use another cup of coffee."

She smiled, nodded and took the cup. He followed her in, quickly scanning the room for more composites. When he saw another, he removed it swiftly, cramming it in with the other. Tina returned with fresh coffee, "Milk and sugar are on the sideboard."

He thanked her and returned to the lobby, now empty, to wait for Richard. He tried to calm himself as he waited, and to some degree was successful. He couldn't decide if he should keep a low profile, or be as visible as any other guest. So far, no one had given him a second glance, being wrapped up in their own enjoyment. The staff was too busy to notice anyone in particular. Visibility here wouldn't be a problem, besides Richard would get upset if he said he was sick, or used some other lame excuse to stay in the room. No, he'd be okay. Most of this crowd was oblivious to him. They felt safe here in the Poconos. Also, he was part of a couple, he fit right in. Still, he'd have to be sure to get rid of any other composites, if there were any.

Richard finally came down, "Good morning, sweetheart," he greeted Antone' as he kissed him. "You were up early."

"I know. I slept very soundly and got up to look at the snow."

Richard turned to look out the window, "It is beautiful. I see they've already plowed and shoveled. We'll go for a walk later, take some pictures."

"That sounds good," Antone' smiled, "Come on, let's eat. I'm hungry." He extended his hands to Richard who pulled him up and they walked into the dining room hand in hand.

Antone' and Richard spent most of the late morning and early afternoon walking along the paths and trails of the resort. By the time they returned to the lodge, the bright sunshine had given way to dark, low hanging clouds. The next storm was moving in. As the sky darkened, so did Antone's mood. He became sullen and withdrawn. He was angry, angry at himself, 'I knew I shouldn't have done it that way. I should have waited, taken my time.'

'No,' he heard, 'If you'd have waited, Marqueth would have hurt you.'

'But now the police know what I did to him, and to the others.'

'No, they only know these men were killed. You're safe from them. And soon you'll get rid of another.'

'I can't. Richard isn't like the others.'

'He is. You can do this, you must.'

Richard asked if he wanted to relax at the small bar adjacent to the dining room and have a brandy before getting ready for the New Year's celebration, Antone' declined. He said he wanted to rest before dinner. Richard asked if he was feeling all right.

"I'm fine, just a little tired, and kind of out of sorts. Maybe I did get up too early this morning. A little nap will put me in better spirits." He looked into Richard's eyes, they looked different, hard and menacing, his handsome features took on an evil continence, and his smile became a sneer. Antone' shook his head, massaging the temples.

"Paul, what's wrong?"

Rubbing his eyes to rid himself of the vision of Richard that he had just seen, he replied, "Dizzy. Must be the change from the cold outside to the warm in here. I'm going upstairs, you go ahead and have a drink. Do you have the key?"

Richard handed it to him, "Do you want something to eat? Maybe it's hunger that made you dizzy. I'm sure I can..."

"No, thanks. I'll be fine." He kissed Richard on the cheek, the stubble pinching his lips. Withdrawing quickly he mounted the stairs. 'See, he's changing. He's starting to drink. Next he'll hurt you, just like the others. You know he will.'

Antone' tried to fight these thoughts, tried to convince himself that what he'd just seen in Richard's face wasn't the real him. 'No, he's different, he won't hurt me,' Antone' argued again.

175

'He will, you know it. You can't give him the chance to hurt you.'

As he unlocked the room, laughter caught his attention. The door to room 7 opened and Tim emerged, followed closely by that other man. "Hi! Enjoying your stay so far?" Tim asked cheerfully.

Antone' nodded and managed a small smile. He watched them bound down the stairs, seemingly happy. 'Don't forget him,' Antone's inner voice hissed. Quickly closing the door behind him, Antone' leaned against it, breathing hard. "I can't, I can't," Antone' repeated over and over again. He threw himself on the bed. Although the sheets were fresh, he smelled stale beer and cigar smoke. The room spun and he could hear those men again, could feel their hands on him, could smell their drunken breath. He pushed their imaginary hands away and pulled himself into a fetal position on the bed, tightly closing his eyes. He could see them now, coming at him, unzipping their pants, laughing as they whooped and cheered each other on. Their heavy bodies, each in turn, using him. He felt the agonizing pain as they entered him and heard their guttural moans as they released themselves in him. Silently he prayed for it to be over, the pain and the humiliation. Finally, with eyes still clamped shut, and covered in sweat and smelling like cigar smoke, he knew they'd finished. He heard them leave, their laughter echoing in his mind.

He opened his eyes. He was alone back in the room, an adult. The darkness was taking him over. He could feel it gaining a foothold on him. He opened his canvass bag and reached in. 'Yes, now you're ready to rid yourself of this man.' He took out the razor sharp hunting knife he'd hidden there. He'd had the knife since childhood, having taken it from his step-father, Marc. Touching it, seeing the glint of light play along its edge calmed him, and took him deeper into the darkness. He slid it under his pillow, knowing it would save him and many others from men like Marc. Finally, his emotions calmed, he slept. In his dreams he has happy, there was no pain, no fear, only the contentment he longed for. There were other young men in his dream, and they were happy too. 'You saved them. You're doing the right thing. Now rest and prepare yourself.'

The storm increased in intensity as the day wore on. Local forecasts predicted as much as another foot by mid-day tomorrow. Residents were being advised to stay indoors and not travel. Many of the side roads were already impassable and the major highways were becoming strewn with abandoned cars. Efforts to keep these roadways passable were becoming more and more difficult as evening approached. Area airports were shut, stranding thousands of would be travelers. So far there were no power outages, but that could change as the winds picked up later in the evening.

Up on Mt. Nebo, things were fine, so far. Staff members had been continually clearing the walkways from the outbuildings to the lodge and the disco, where the New Year's Eve celebration was to be held. No one seemed particularly concerned about the raging storm. Some of the guests had already inquired about extending their stay a day or two. Charlie told Tim and Stacy to offer a 20% discount to anyone who wanted, or needed to stay.

"What if they're short on cash, or don't have a credit card?" Tim asked, knowing the policy of the lodge had always been not to accept personal checks.

"Those would be a small minority. Ask for a small deposit and tell them that we'll bill them for the balance, but don't make that offer unless they're really in need of it. Try to stick to our standard policy as much as possible."

"Maybe we should take personal checks. I mean this is kind of an unusual situation. Could we make an exception to the policy?"

"God, I don't know. The previous owners never did that before, I don't want to set a precedent. What do you think, Jonathan?"

Jonathan thought for a moment, "Considering the circumstances, I think we should. Most of these people are return guests. I'm sure there won't be a problem. But, only as a last resort."

Those decisions made, they went back to their own work. Tim remained at the front desk extending stays for guests, Charlie headed for the kitchen to check supplies for the unexpected extensions. They were in good shape and wouldn't run short of much, maybe orange juice, and sausage for breakfast, and an outside chance of running low on chicken. If the roads didn't open up in a day or two, however, they'd be in real trouble. Jonathan, meanwhile, circulated among the tables in the packed dining room, informing guests of the weather situation and reassuring them that they could stay as long as necessary. Most were grateful, but a few thought they should be allowed to stay for free. Jonathan simply smiled and told these guests that he wished that was possible and excused himself.

Harold and the rest of NuView had already eaten and were resting before their performance. The show ran almost 2 hours, so they had to start before 10:00 to be finished as the New Year arrived.

At 8:30 he roused everyone. They took turns showering and had a small snack and drink, no alcohol, before bundling up for the short but frigid walk to the disco. Ron and Anthony were ready first and waited in the living room, munching chips and drinking sodas. Harold was with them, having his usual, coffee and a peanut butter sandwich. Looking out the picture window he shook his head, "This is never going to stop. I haven't seen snow like this since the early 90's".

"How long do you think we'll have to stay here?" Anthony asked.

Taking a sip of coffee, Harold turned to them and shrugged, "I don't know. Two maybe three days."

Anthony looked at Ron, and taking his hands, said, "How about making this our honeymoon?"

Ron stared at him in disbelief, Harold choked on his sandwich. "For real?"

"Yes, for real. I want us to be together for the rest of our lives, and I can't think of a better place and time to make that commitment to each other. What do you say?"

Ron nodded and grabbed Anthony, hugging him as tightly as he could, tears of joy streaking his face.

Ray and Steve heard the commotion and came running in, Steve still dripping from the shower. "What's wrong? What happened? Why is Ron crying? Is he hurt?"

"No," Harold said, still stunned, but happy for them. "Unless my hearing is totally gone, Anthony just asked Ron to be his lover. I guess you were right about the two of them all along, Steve."

Ray and Steve looked at each other, mouths agape, then congratulated Ron and Anthony. The small room became totally silent as everyone let the news sink in, then they broke into spontaneous laughter. Suddenly, Steve realized he was standing there totally naked. "Holy shit!" he exclaimed as he grabbed a cushion from the sofa and ran to his room to dress.

Ray rolled his eyes. "Like we all haven't seen that before!" he smirked.

Chapter 15 — NEW YEARS EVE

The crowded dining room swirled around Antone', voices sounded muffled and distant. He found it difficult to concentrate on anything, his meal, the conversation, even what Jonathan had said when he stopped by their table. His mind was in that other place, far from the here and now. Locked within his mind memories of another New Year's Eve came flooding back to him.

He was in his room at home, hiding under the covers as the partying and drinking continued downstairs. Most of the guests had gone home, but his step-father's cronies stayed. He heard footsteps, his door knob rattle, then slowly open. Fearing the worst, he cringed under the heavy comforter, but it was his mother. She came to her son and, smelling of cigarette smoke and whiskey, leaned over him. He felt her warm hands on his head, and heard her drunken slur, "Happy New Year, sweetie." She kissed his forehead as gently as she could then staggered out. Why couldn't she see what was happening? How could she let him do this to him? How could she have married him so soon after his father's death? Silently he cried out to her, "Please, Mommy. Please make him stop!" but he never said anything to her, couldn't bring himself to say the words out loud. He simply suffered in silence. Everything was quiet for a while and he thought his step-father might have forgotten, or passed out on the couch, maybe, but no, shortly he heard the footsteps, and knew it was going to happen again.

Another memory flashed through his tormented mind. He was 14, tall and getting strong by using a set of free weights he'd found in the basement. He started working out regularly and liked the way he looked, so did others, boys as well as girls.   He enjoyed the flirtations of both sexes and by the time he was a high school junior had experienced sex with both. Sex with girls was good, but with a boy he found himself reaching higher levels of satisfaction. Maybe it was the feeling of a boy's firmness, maybe it was the sameness of their bodies, maybe it was the power he felt.   He didn't know, or care, he wanted it, had to have the feeling of power and conquest over another boy.

As he grew taller and stronger, his step-father grew older. He watched and waited, knowing he'd have his turn soon to humiliate and hurt this man worse than he'd ever been hurt.   His opportunity came on his step-father's 40th birthday. He sullenly watched as Marc and his circle of friends predictably got drunk, knowing that this celebration would follow the pattern of the past 7 to 8 years. He was ready for it, all his childhood fear of this man had been replaced with anger, hatred, and the need for revenge. As the party wound down, Marc came over and sat next to his step-son, "You ready to give me what I want, boy?"

Staring straight ahead he replied in a cold voice, "Oh yeah. I've got what you want, all right, but," he looked directly into Marc's bloodshot, puffy eyes, "How about just you and me this time? After all, it is your 40th birthday."

Marc was delighted, "That's a great idea. You'll be all mine and I won't have to wait for the others to finish with you. I can have you as much as I want." Marc rose unsteadily to his feet and found his way to his small circle of friends. They glared over at Antone' as Marc told them of the special night he was going to have alone with his step-son. He watched as they slowly nodded and left.

Later that evening, his wife drunk and snoring loudly in their room, Marc came to Antone's bedroom. Closing and locking the door behind him, he crept to the bed and crawled onto his step-son's body. He had sobered up a bit, but was still pretty drunk. Biting Antone's neck and chest, they never kissed, Marc noticed with heightened delight at how aroused Antone' was. This increased his intensity and caused the boy to bite back, hard. Marc winced and pulled back. "Sorry, I'm just so turned on tonight, knowing it's just you and me." Grasping the boy's thick erection he inhaled, "I can tell."

Antone' moved his legs slightly apart, as if preparing for Marc's entry. While Marc was probing, Antone' slowly raised his outside leg and reversed positions, pinning Marc with his strong hands. "What the hell do you think you're doing?" Marc protested.

Putting one finger to his lips, Antone' quieted his step-father, "Why giving you your birthday present!" he grinned and began nibbling Marc's body while slowly rotating his hips. Soon Marc was lost in the pleasurable sensations he was feeling, "Oh, yeah. Go ahead, get your head down there," he groaned, but Antone' had different ideas. He spit generously into his palm and lubricated himself, then in one hard flowing motion raised Marc's legs and plunged into him.

Marc let out a scream of pain, horror and disbelief. He thrashed wildly, struggling to get free, but his hands were pinned tightly to the bed as Antone' pumped brutally into him. "What's wrong, Dad? Don't you like your present?" he asked as he pumped harder, knowing he was hurting Marc.

Marc began railing obscenities, but his words were unheard. Antone's eyes were enraged, all the anger, hate, humiliation and fear focused on this act. Feeling his climax building, Antone' pulled out of his step-father's bruised and bloody body and spewed himself onto Marc's chest and face. Marc lie there motionless, every nerve ending in his body flamed white hot with pain. Totally being controlled now, Marc felt himself being pulled off the bed and roughly shoved down the hall into the bathroom, the fear visible on his ashen face. Seeing this aroused Antone' again and he sneered, "Does it hurt? Oh, poor Marc." Laughing evilly, he grabbed Marc by the arms so hard they bruised, and threw him into the shower. Turning on the water full blast, he stepped in behind him. Using the soap to lather his throbbing erection, he used Marc again, pinning him to the cold tile of the shower. This time he released himself into Marc. As he came, he pulled Marc's head back by the hair and grunted, "Do you feel it? Hot, isn't it? You're such a good bitch!" then withdrew. Completely traumatized, Marc slumped to the floor of the shower, convulsing. Antone' washed himself, keeping a wary eye of the heaving figure at his feet.

Snapping up and back without warning, Marc sent his step-son sprawling to the back of the shower. He groped his way out of the bathroom and onto the second floor hallway. Antone' recovered quickly, enraged by this act. Overcoming the older man in a few steps, he spun Marc around to face him, "Oh no you don't. I'm not finished with you yet!" Marc began swinging his fists wildly, landing a few blows, splitting Antone's lip. Staggering back a few steps, Antone' tasted the coppery blood and saw it on his finger tips. "You son of a bitch!" he howled as he lunged towards Marc. Leaning on the railing for support, Marc tried to turn and run, but his feet slipped on the wet, hardwood floor and he screamed. Antone' watched as Marc hurtled, in slow motion, to the tile floor below, arms and legs flailing. He struck the floor forcefully, a crimson pool instantly forming around his head. Staggering out of her room, Antone's mother screamed when she saw the broken form of her husband on the floor below, and her only son standing at the rail, naked and dripping wet. "How in God's name did this happen?!" she bellowed. Antone' looked her directly in the eye, his face calm, and without showing a bit of emotion in his voice said, "He slipped. I guess the floor was wet after I took my shower," and returned to his room,

The death was ruled accidental.

Slowly the present crept back, like the rising sun burning off the morning mist, and he could again hear the conversations around him and see the people who were having them. A voice caught his attention as a hand grasped his wrist, it was Richard. "Paul! Are you all right?"

"Huh? Oh, yeah," he fumbled. "Sorry, I guess I got caught up in my own thoughts."

Releasing his wrist, Richard agreed, "I'll say. You were staring into space for quite a while. I was beginning to get worried. You're sure there's nothing wrong?"

Antone' shook his head then noticed the table had been cleared. "Where's my dinner?"

Richard looked surprised, "The waiter just cleared the plates. He asked you if you were done and you nodded, so he took your plate."

"Wow! I really was away, wasn't I? I'm sorry." He looked at Richard but saw Marc's face and heard his voice.

"You ready for dessert? You can get anything you want."

Antone' pulled back shaking his head, "What? What did you just say?"

191

"Paul," Richard was getting angry, "All I asked was if you were going to have dessert. Maybe you should have a drink, I think you need one, I know I do."

The darkness was there sinking deeper into him, he saw everything differently now. He heard it in Richard's voice, saw it in his face. It was growing and there was little he could do to stop it now.

When the waiter returned for their dessert order, Antone' asked for coffee, nothing else. Sipping the hot coffee and staring at Richard over the rim of the cup he felt...rage? anger? fear? disgust? He couldn't tell, but it was there. Everything was there now, all the signs he had been dreading finally fell into place, and the darkness took him over fully. Richard was just like the rest. A slight grin curled Antone's lip and he heard, 'Punish him. You can see him for what he is now. He's Marc. He's your parish priest. He's all of them. Stop him. Do it tonight, before he hurts you like they did.'

Antone's eyes glared as he mumbled his response. "I will. I certainly will."

Richard finished his drink. How many had he drunk? Three? Four? Looking at his watch he said, "We'd better hurry if we want to get a table for the show. It starts in less than an hour now."

Rising, Antone' made an excuse to return to their room, "I want to change before we go. I'm going to put on a sweater. It's more comfortable and I don't want your jacket smelling like cigarette smoke, or getting drinks spilled on it." Exasperated, Richard told him to go, he'd wait here having another drink. Once alone inside the room, Antone' removed the hunting knife from beneath his pillow. He had to see it once more tonight to calm himself. The cold, hard blade, so cool to the touch, soothed him. He ran the flat side of the blade across his cheek, feeling the smoothness of the fine steel. This was a good choice, an appropriate choice for what used to be a hunting lodge. He laughed at his own cynicism. He returned the knife, straightened out the bed and began changing. 'I'm proud of you,' he heard, 'you made the right choice, you'll see. Soon you'll be safe again.'

Antone' smiled at his reflection in the mirror. He knew now that the voice he heard was right, he had to do this, he had no other choice.

Richard had finished his drink and was waiting for him in the lobby. "What took you so long? I hope we can still get a table. I certainly don't want to stand throughout this show!" They put on their coats and left the lodge, pushing past other guests on the slippery walk.

There were a few small tables left near the far side of the dance floor that was serving as the stage. Richard took Antone' by the hand and quickly led him to one. There was no table service and Richard asked what he wanted to drink. "Just get me a soda. I don't think I ate too much and would get drunk very fast."

"Suit yourself." Richard replied curtly and went to the bar. Antone' looked around the club. The room was large and open. A pool table stood in the far left, behind where they were sitting, pinball machines were lined up over to the far right. The bar itself was a 10' by 10' square just off center of the room. Mini lights twinkled around the entire perimeter of the large room. He saw the d.j. booth opposite their table and the rest rooms just beyond it. Richard returned with their drinks and after a few sips, Antone' said he was going to hit the men's room before the show started.

Crossing over the dance floor he felt good, the calm peacefulness he'd always experienced settling over him like a cocoon. His calm was momentarily ruffled, however, when he saw another police composite on the wall near the rest rooms. He thought about tearing this one down too then realized that nobody was paying the least bit of attention to it, or to him, so why bother. He returned to the table feeling better by the minute. Just before the show started he noticed Richard staring at him, his eyes hard and cold, "What?" he asked.

"Nothing," Richard said with a wave of his hand.

"Richard, what's wrong?"

Through a slurred voice, Richard asked if he was having a good time.

A bit surprised by the question, Antone' responded enthusiastically, "My God, yes. This has been wonderful" he leaned over and kissed Richard on the cheek, "Thank you, very much."

Richard's eyes softened a little and he returned the kiss, "You are very welcome."

The smell of alcohol reached Antone's brain just as the lights dimmed for the start of the show. In the dwindling light he heard, 'Oh yes, just like Marc.'

Chapter 16 — THE SHOW

The performance went along spectacularly. Harold's comedy routines were current, quick and cuttingly funny. By the time he finished his first set, the audience was anxiously awaiting more, and they got it.

Ron's first set of illusions went flawlessly. He flowed from one to another seamlessly, delighting everyone. Anthony, awaiting his turn, watched from behind the makeshift curtain the staff had put up.

"My God, he's good tonight!" he whispered to Harold, who was standing behind him.

"Of course he is," Harold replied, putting his hands on Anthony's shoulders, "He's in love." Anthony grinned widely and turned to kiss Harold on his plump cheek. "Well, looks like he's wrapping this up. I'd better get out there to announce you." Harold swept through the curtain, hands help high. "Isn't he marvelous?" he asked an already enthusiastic audience. Ron bowed and started to back off stage, but Harold stopped him, "Not so fast, honey," he whispered. Taking Ron's arm, he quieted the audience and stepped forward. A puzzled murmuring swept through the crowd of about 300, they knew this wasn't part of the show. Backstage, Anthony was confused as well. Ray and Steve, who had just come out of the dressing room wanted to know why it was so quiet, and what Harold was saying. "Damned if I know," Anthony told them. They all listened intently to see what Harold was up to.

"They say that when you go looking for love, you never find it. But when you stop looking, you do, usually right in your own backyard." He now had everyone's attention, even the bartenders stopped mixing and serving drinks. "Well, tonight, just before the show, Ron here stopped searching," he turned towards the curtain, "Anthony, darling, front and center. Mother Merman needs you."

"I don't believe he's doing this." Anthony said as he stepped onto the stage. Taking his arm, so he was flanked by Ron and Anthony, Harold continued. "And this is who he found. His best friend, confidant, and soul mate." Harold stood back and pushed Ron and Anthony together. Coming around them he proudly announced, "These two gorgeous men have decided to make a commitment to each other. Everyone, pick up your glass." Turning his attention to the bar, he called for three glasses of champagne. Taking one for himself and handing the other two to an already embarrassed Ron and Anthony, he toasted them. "Here's to a new year, a new millennium, and a new beginning. I love you both." Everyone drank then applauded the two men. Someone started clinking their glass and soon the room was filled with the sound. Ron and Anthony kissed in response then thanked everyone. Suddenly, Ron grabbed Anthony's arm tightly, causing him to wince. When the applause died down, Harold got on with the show by introducing Anthony, and escorting Ron off stage.

Anthony's voice was a bit shaky at first, but he performed wonderfully. When he finished, and the applause died down, he thanked the audience for their show of love and support and exited the stage as Harold came on for his second comedy set.

He pulled Ron aside the moment he got back stage. "What is going on with you?" Anthony asked, "You almost cut off the circulation in my arm out there!"

"He's here! Right out in front!"

"What the hell are you taking about? Who's here?"

"The murderer! The one in the picture I showed you."

"What? You're seeing things. What would he be doing here of all places?"

Pushing Anthony to the curtain and opening it a crack he nervously told him, "Just look, third table on the left, with the older man."

Anthony peeked out and saw who Ron was referring to. "It looks like the guy in the drawing, but you can't be that certain, Ron. I mean, be reasonable, what are the odds of him showing up here in the Poconos? He's a city boy, remember?

"I know what the police bulletin said!" Ron snapped, "But I know it's him, and I know I've seen him before. It didn't make sense until I saw him with that older gentleman. I thought, 'What is a good-looking, young man like that doing with someone old enough to be his father?' That snapped everything into focus. He's the same guy I saw when we performed in Denver last summer. He was with an older man then, and I had the same thought."

"Ron, look, a lot's happened tonight, you're probably overcome by it all. Come on, let me help you get ready for your finale. If you still think it's him after you're done, we'll go to Jonathan and Charlie and have them get in touch with the police, okay?"

Ron agreed and they went off to get him ready for his last illusion. By the time he went on, Ron was somewhat calmer, a second glass of champagne helped. The lights went off, Ron silently got in place, and as the music began and the blue overhead stage lights rose slightly, he began his strip. First the elbow length evening gloves were seductively removed and casually dropped on tables, then the earrings and necklace, these he gave to the butchest lesbian he could see for her to guard. Part of the success of this illusion was Ron's uncanny ability to make and hold direct eye contact with people, pulling them into his fantasy.

As the illusion progressed, and the smoke began to rise, he moved to the far side of the stage and played to the people standing along the wall near the rest rooms. A disembodied face caught his eye, the police composite, right there. Without thinking, he turned his attention to the left side of the stage and stared directly into Antone's eyes. It was him, no doubt about it now. The smoke became thicker and slowly rose, why was it taking so long? Finally it was to his neck, he moved into the thickest part of it and unhooked the bra, his gaze fixed on Antone' again just as the lights went out.

"He knows!" Antone' thought, and his heart began pounding. Looking at the cheering audience, he saw the composite, that one damned paper he didn't destroy, now mocked him. How could he have been so smug! He wanted to run, but there was no place to go. Calming himself, he decided that Ron, too, must go. That was a pity, but unavoidable now. He knew there was no rush, even if the police were called it would take several hours for them to get here. While NuView took their final curtain calls, he formulated a plan.

Jonathan and Charlie stepped up to the stage. "Everyone, it's time!" Charlie excitedly called over the din. Noise makers, hats, and champagne were handed out. Jonathan nodded to the d.j. who started the countdown, with everyone soon joining in. At midnight, balloons dropped from the ceiling, confetti was thrown, noisemakers cranked and paper horns blew. Couples hugged and kissed, so did strangers. It was 2000, not only a new year, but a new millennium, fraught with fear, anticipation and hope. The traditional Auld Lang Zine was sung, and then the real party began. Allowing himself to be hugged and kissed by strangers as well as Richard, who was quite drunk now, Antone' never let Ron stray far from sight. At one point he noticed him talking to Anthony, who glanced over in his direction. They were soon surrounded by people congratulating them.

A lavish buffet was spread on the covered pool table. Antone' quickly grabbed some sandwiches to eat now, and others to wrap up for later. Shortly before 1:30 he convinced Richard that they should leave to, 'celebrate in private'. The short walk to the lodge was perilous, although the wind had diminished somewhat, the snow was still falling in blinding sheets. Richard needed some help, but was surprisingly steady on his feet, the cold air rousing him.

Once in their room, Antone' quickly stashed the stolen food in his bag, undressed and got into bed, Richard soon followed. Antone' allowed himself to be groped, fondled and kissed despite the revulsion he felt from the alcohol on Richard's breath and the smell of stale cigarette smoke on his body. Antone' waited, flashes of the past piercing through like a series of snapshots, heightening his darkness, preparing him for what he knew he had to do. There was no voice now, none was necessary, he was poised, looking for the signs he knew so well, the glassy eyed glare of the animal inside all such men, the need to dominate and hurt.

Richard's excitement grew and he began breathing heavily and sweating, the sour perspiration mixing with the alcohol and smoke, nauseating Antone'. Finally, Richard rolled over on top of him, grinding his hips, forcing Antone's legs apart, his hard throbbing erection pulsing and ready. Pushing himself up onto his palms, Richard glared down lustfully at Antone', who saw the look he was waiting for. In a drunken slur, Richard uttered the words that sealed his fate, "You ready to give me what I want, boy?"

The darkness inside Antone' was replaced with a blinding white hate. His eyes blazed with it, his lips curled back, and his chest heaved. Reaching beneath his pillow, he found the knife. Grasping it firmly by the shaft, he brought it out and as Richard saw the light reflect off of the blade, he brought it up and slashed at Richard's throat in one swift motion. Shock and agony shot across Richard's face as hot blood instantly sprayed across the room. Antone' slashed again, completely severing his throat, the pulsing blood coating the bed, walls and him. Finally, gurgling his last breath, Richard collapsed, dead on top of him.

Antone' extricated himself from the blood soaked bed and stood there, naked and covered in blood. He stared at the body, now lying on its back, mouth agape, eyes wide, the flow of blood slowing, trying to clot the fatal wound. He didn't move, didn't blink. He studied the body, it was hard to believe this was the remains of a man that would have hurt him, humiliated him. As his breathing returned to normal, he heard, 'Another one removed,' and smiled. Finally calmed, he looked at himself and frowned, "Oh my God!" he said aloud. He used the small sink in the room to wash the knife, and himself. He washed hard, scrubbing his skin raw. He used every towel and washcloth to scrub the blood from his body, and after inspecting himself thoroughly for any trace of blood, packed up. He couldn't take Richard's money, credit cards, or what little jewelry there was. He was about to leave the room when he remembered the car keys. Even though the snow was deep, and roads blocked, the car would be there for him to use as soon as possible, hopefully by morning. After finding them in Richard's coat pocket, he placed the 'DO NOT DISTURB' sign on the door, and left the lodge. He had to get away, not for fear of being caught, but from the fear of what he'd done, again.

He located Richard's car and put his bag in the trunk. Before closing it, he checked the amount of food he'd taken.   Deciding it wasn't enough he opened the driver's door and took the plastic shopping bag Richard used for litter from around the cigarette lighter. He emptied it and turned it inside out and stuck it in his pocket, next to the knife, now safely in its sheath. Heading back to the disco, he noticed the snow was letting up, a good sign.

It was well past 2:00 A.M. when he returned to the disco, but the party was still in full swing. He was pleased to see the buffet table still had a good amount of food left, and that there was now fresh fruit and desserts. He filled a plate and at the same time was able to fill his coat pockets. Standing in the corner eating, he searched the crowd, but there was no sign of the young entertainer who'd recognized him. He did, however, spot that other man, his arm around his young friend, happy and blissfully ignorant of his fate. Antone' milled through the crowd, eating everything on his plate then returning for more. The darkness taking him over again.

Gary and Tim prepared to leave a short time later. Noticing this, Antone' excused himself from a rather drunk man who had struck up some sort of conversation, claiming he wanted to get back to his other half, who he'd left sleeping, and edged his way to the door. Being sure to stay back a bit, he followed the couple, unsheathing and removing the knife as he did.

The path to the lodge, although not deep with snow, was slippery. Gary and Tim held onto each other as they carefully picked their way to the lodge. Antone' kept his head down as he gained on the unsuspecting men, preparing to strike his second victim before seeking out the entertainer who'd identified him. He was within inches of being able to strike. He positioned the blade to sink deep into Gary's back, plunging it upwards, on the left side into the heart. A scream and peal of laughter caused Tim and Gary to turn, Antone's blow missed its fatal mark and instead sunk partly into Gary's right side, under the ribs. Gary let out a muffled grunt as his hands went to his side. Tim screamed as he slumped into the snow, Antone' already a blur in the dark, snowy night. Tim's calls for help alerted the 2 women who, moments before, were enjoying the snow and the holiday. They ran to the fallen man.

"What happened?" one of the women asked as she knelt down in the snow.

"I don't know." Tim stuttered, "I think that guy hit him." Then, taking Gary's hand, he felt the slick, warm blood. "Oh my God! He's bleeding! Somebody get help!"

One woman ran back to the disco while the other ripped open Gary's shirt. Seeing the wound, she looked up at Tim, "He's been stabbed." She immediately packed some fresh snow on the wound to help stop the bleeding. Gary's breath was shallow and he was staring straight ahead. "Give me your coat." She said to Tim.

"What?"

"Give, me, your, coat!" she repeated, reaching her hand to him. "He could be going into shock, but I think he'll be okay. What's his name?"

"Gary."

"Gary!" she called, patting his face. "Look at me. You'll be all right. Just stay with me." She turned to Tim, "You work here, don't you?" He nodded. "Go up to the lodge and get blankets. We can't risk moving him yet, but we've got to keep him as warm as we can. And get towels and bandages if you can." Tim sat in the snow motionless. "Hurry! Go!" she yelled. Tim stumbled up to the lodge, still in shock himself. By the time he returned, there was a crowd at the scene. Jonathan saw Tim returning and went to help him. Seeing Jonathan approaching, Tim thought the worst. "Is he...?"

Putting his arm around Tim, Jonathan assured him that Gary was going to be fine. "Come on, he's asking for you."

Leslie took the blankets and small first aid kit from Tim. She removed the coats that had been covering Gary and, using towels and the bottle of betadine, cleaned the area around the wound. "The bleeding has slowed a great deal." she said to them, then went to work using the minimal supply of sterile gauze and adhesive tape to dress the wound. She covered him with the clean blankets then leaned back. Looking up at Jonathan, she asked if they had a stretcher, they didn't. "We've got to get him indoors and take off these wet clothes."

"How about one of the plywood sheets we used to cover the pool table with?"

"Go! Was all Leslie said.

In a relatively short time they had Gary on the board and up to the lodge, Tim holding his hand the whole way. They laid him on the sofa in the lobby and Leslie again checked for fresh bleeding, she was relieved not to find any. "How are you feeling?" she asked Gary, whose color was slowly returning.

"I could use a drink! A stiff one!" The crowd, which stayed with them, sighed a tension breaking laugh.

"Not a bad idea. I sure as hell could use one!" Leslie replied smiling, her hands trembling now that the immediate crisis seemed to be over.

Charlie and Jonathan went to the small bar in the dining room and returned with glasses and bottles of whiskey, gin, vodka, and wine, anyone who wanted a drink could have one or two. Slowly the crowd dwindled, exhaustion taking over. By the time the sun started rising, there were only 4 people remaining, Leslie and her girlfriend, who were dozing on a lobby sofa. Tim who was sitting on the piano stool, rocking back and forth, and of course Gary, who had drifted off to sleep an hour or so ago. Charlie and Jonathan were near the dining room door, talking in whispered voices. "Ron was right." Charlie said.

"I know. I wish he'd said something to us sooner."

"Well, at least you were able to get a call through to Agent Atkinson. I just hope to God he can get help here soon, if at all."

Although the snow had slowed to a flurry, the wind had picked up and piled drifts everywhere. It could take hours for any help to arrive. Through red, swollen eyes Tim noticed their conversation, "What are you two talking about?"

Picking their words carefully, they told Tim about the information they'd received from Ron DuBuois, and that they managed to get a call through to the F.B.I. agent Jonathan's father knew.

Tim refused to believe that the serial killer the police were looking for was here. "No, that's not possible! I checked the reservations myself, there wasn't a Z last name in the entire lot of them. Here, I'll show you." Angrily, Tim pulled out the reservation cards from behind the front desk and started going through them.

"Tim, don't. We didn't mean any..." Jonathan stopped mid word as Tim's face went ashen and tears streamed down his cheeks. "What's wrong? Tim! Answer me! What did you find?"

Charlie took the card from Tim's shaking hand. The reservation had been made under the name

Richard Pauley, of Pittsburgh, but at the bottom, on the line for a guest to sign, was the name Paul Zimza. Dumbfounded, he handed the card to Jonathan. Tim was already blaming himself, "This is my fault. I had the card in my hand." He told Charlie and Jonathan that a couple, an older and younger man, were the last to register, and how Stacy had been taunting him about Gary. "I just didn't look at the name, and now..." he looked at Gary and went to pieces.

While Jonathan did his best to comfort Tim, Charlie checked the room number and went up. Seeing the 'DO NOT DISTURB' sign on the door he was reluctant to knock. He returned to the lobby and told them about the sign on the door.

"What about the car? Is it still here?"

Jonathan checked the registration card for the make and model of car, then went to the edge of the porch to look for it. "It's still here. But there's very little snow on the trunk. The hood and roof are piled like the other cars, but there's just an inch or so on the trunk."

"You don't think there's a body in there, do you?" Tim asked.

Jonathan and Charlie looked at each other. "We've got to check that room. Get the extra key." Jonathan headed towards the stairs as Charlie retrieved it. "Tim, you stay here with Gary, and listen for the phone," he called as he took the stairs 2 at a time.

By the time he got to room 6, Jonathan had already knocked several times without getting any response. "Open it."

Charlie quickly unlocked and opened the door. An other worldly odor struck them. Jonathan clicked on the lights and they both gasped at the grotesque scene in front of them. The body lay on its back, eyes and mouth open wide, the slashed throat caked with blood. One hand clutched at the fatal wound, as if trying to stop the flow, the other was outstretched, grasping for help. The bed was sodden with dark, drying blood, and the walls dripped with it. Bloody towels were strewn about the small room, and the sink was stained crimson with it. Neither man could move, there was so much blood, so much gore.

Charlie recovered a bit, "Jesus Christ!" he moaned, then started to move into the room.

"No!" Jonathan grabbed him. "We can't go in there. This is a crime scene now. We could disturb evidence."

Charlie looked at him confused. Jonathan shrugged, "Hey, my dad's a cop."

Chapter 17 — JANUARY 1st

Antone' woke with a start, not knowing where he was or why he was there. As he looked around the small, cold cabin, his head cleared and he slowly remembered the events of the night before. Richard was gone and he was safe again. He suddenly sat up straight in the single bed, the other man, could he have survived? Antone' fought to remember the events of that incident. He saw the man, heard the laughter behind him and could actually feel the blade sink into the man's body. Yes, he was dead, bled to death in the snow. His young boyfriend would cry and grieve the loss for a while, but would realize that he had been saved from the hurt and pain that would surely be inflicted upon him. He sunk back into the bed, pulling the light spread to his neck. He'd be safe here for a while, probably all day, if not longer. He turned his thoughts to the young entertainer who recognized him. "Strange," he thought, "I don't know now if I need to eliminate him. I was so sure last night, but now he doesn't matter, isn't important. I'll think about him more later."

He pulled a sandwich from his coat pocket. The bread was a little stale, and salami and cheese wasn't exactly breakfast fare, but he was hungry. He ate 2 sandwiches and an apple. Checking his jacket pockets he saw that he had a few more sandwiches and another apple and an orange left. Later, after dark, he'd sneak back to the car and retrieve his bag for the rest of the food he had, and his tooth brush. His stomach reasonable full, and his mind at ease, he soon fell back to sleep.

By 11:00, the sun finally broke through and guest started emerging to clear off their cars. They made fun out of it, hurling snow at each other and making snowmen and women after they were done. They knew leaving was impossible, no plows had been through yet, but they enjoyed their situation, many taking photos of other guests and the winter wonderland scenery that surrounded them. No one had any knowledge of the gruesome scene in room 6, Jonathan and Charlie had told only Tim and swore him to secrecy. They had all gotten some sleep, but were dragging through the day.

Gary was quite sore, but much better by mid-afternoon. He wanted to sit up, but Leslie wouldn't let him, knowing he'd open up the wound and start bleeding again. When Gary protested, saying he had to use the bathroom, she brought him an empty plastic soda bottle. "Use this," she told him, stifling a laugh.

"Right here? In the lobby?"

"It's either this, or hold it."

Turning red as a beet, he took the 2 liter bottle and motioned for her to turn around, or better yet, leave the room. He'd give the bottle to Tim to empty.

Leslie woke Tim, who'd fallen asleep in the arm chair near Gary, and told him the situation. He looked over at Gary who waved the still empty bottle at him. Looking back at Leslie he nodded. She went into the dining room for coffee and to get Gary some clear soup and bread.

Tim patiently waited and took the bottle from Gary when he had finished. Leslie returned with a tray holding a large styrofoam cup, a straw and two slices of bread, Tim was close behind carrying the now empty bottle. She inserted the straw into the cup and held it out to Gary. "Can I at least prop up a little?" he implored, "I can't drink lying down." She put the cup down on the tray and got a pillow. "You," she said firmly, pointing at Gary, "Do not try to help by pulling yourself up. We'll maneuver you. Tim, give me a hand." Together they moved Gary up a bit and made sure he was comfortable. Before she let him have the soup, Leslie took his temperature, it was normal. "Well, that's a good sign. There doesn't appear to be any sign of infection." She reached for the tray again. "Take the cup and sip slowly, it's hot."

Gary took a long sip, then a bit of the bread, "Good," was all he said, and he continued sipping the soup and eating the bread. All the while, Tim sat watching Gary, tears filling his eyes then flowing down his cheeks, he made no attempt to wipe them away. Gary looked at him, Leslie following his eyes, she knew when to back out. "Tim, see that he finishes this and maybe some ice cream or jello if he wants. I've got to get some rest." Tim hurriedly wiped his face and nodded. Leslie started toward the stairs, but Gary called to her, "Leslie, I don't know how to thank you. You saved my life."

She smiled and quipped, "Dedicate your next book to me."

"You know me?" Gary was surprised, he never thought of himself as a known author.

"I've read both your books. Knew you right away."

"You got it! If it wasn't for you, there'd be no next book."

She smiled and left Gary and Tim alone, knowing they needed to talk.

The sound of snow plows woke Antone'. It was already starting to get dark, but the rotating orange lights of the plows cut through the gathering darkness as their steel blades scraped the snow from the roads. "Good," he thought, "I'll be able to get out of here soon." He stretched and got out of bed, rubbing his arms against the cold. He pulled the remaining food from his coat and ate quickly, anxious to get moving. What he couldn't know, however, was that the plows, in addition to removing the snow were bringing in state police. Dressed in everyday clothes, the two men and two women would pose as guests. The men were to be the decoys in this operation, acting as a couple, one older, one younger, trying to lure the murderer to act again. They knew he was still on the grounds, there was no way he could have left yet, but they also knew that if he was hiding somewhere on the grounds he'd soon grow restless, and hungry. They hoped that this combination and seeing a younger man with an older one would lure him out into the open, and make a mistake. The male officers were to make themselves as visible as possible, especially outside. 'Paul', as they now knew the murderer, would be watching from somewhere, he could even be walking around the grounds like any of the other guests, especially since no one recognized him except Ron.

The first thing the team did was to investigate and photograph the crime scene, and dust for prints. This had to be done as quickly and discreetly as possible, none of the guests were aware of the murder, and as far as Gary's stabbing was concerned, they'd been told, at the urging of the police, to say it was a jealous former lover who went into a drunken rage at seeing his ex with someone new.

Removal of the body would be extremely difficult to do undetected. After many incomplete ideas, a decision was made to wrap the body in all the bed clothes, along with the bloody towels and lower it out the rear window fire escape of the lodge. It could then be carried down to and kept in the tool shed in the back until it could be properly cared for.

Those items having been taken care of, they next turned their attention to the victim and his background. Using his registration card as a starting point, they contacted Police Headquarters in Pittsburgh, and asked them to investigate Richard's activities since November. They were also asked to recirculate the composite using the new alias, Paul Zimza, "Have it run in local newspapers and on the evening news. He has to have left some kind of paper trail." Hanging up, Sergeant Caputo now wanted to meet with Ron to see if he could add any details to the composite they'd been circulating, maybe there was something not quite right enough with it to make others recognize him.

On his way to the office to meet with Ron and refine the composite, Sgt. Caputo stopped to see how Gary was doing. Leslie, the E.M.T. who was tending to Gary's wound asked if and when an ambulance might be able to get through to take him to a hospital.

Caputo rubbed the back of his neck, "I honestly don't know what to tell you. The road crews have been swamped, as you can imagine. This road," he gestured to Mt. Nebo Road, "is barely a secondary road. I can call the local road department, tell them it's an emergency, but I doubt an ambulance would be able to get here until late tonight. Will he be okay that long?"

Leslie nodded. "He should be fine. It's really a bit more serious than a flesh wound. I'm worried about infection setting in, especially since it's too late for stitches."

"I'll see what I can do for you, Leslie. By the way, thanks for all your help in this."

"Glad I was here to help." She responded and went back to changing the dressing on Gary's wound.

Ron came to the lodge's small office with Anthony. He was still shaken by the whole ordeal, but wanted to help in any way he could. Sergeant Caputo showed him the composite. "Mr. DuBuois, what I need you to do is help us refine this drawing, bring it more into focus so he's more readily identifiable."

Ron took the sketch and studied it. "Well, the shape of the face is a bit too full, it should be thinner and a bit more angular. And the eyes should be deeper set and rounder, and he has dark circles under his eyes, like he doesn't sleep much." He studied it again as Caputo finished noting what he'd already said.

"Anything else?"

A long silence.

"Honey? Anthony asked, "Are you okay?"

Ron nodded, then his eyes widened, "The nose, that's what else is wrong." He turned the drawing to face the sergeant. "Look, in the sketch, his nose is straight from top to tip, it isn't. There's a bend in it, it's crooked, like it had been broken, you know? Like some boxers' noses. It bends to the left, I think. Yes, to the left, from about here," he pointed to the center of the bridge, "down."

They worked together on the new composite for over an hour. When it was finished, the subtle differences Ron had pointed out brought a new realism to the face. "That's him! That's the guy I saw in Denver and here last night!"

Concerned by the palor in Ron's face, Anthony softly asked, "Are you sure?"

Ron nodded. He was both excited and frightened by the pencil sketch that stared lifelessly at him. "If only I'd done something sooner," he said softly.

Sergeant Caputo assured him that he'd done more than he could imagine. He then turned to Charlie, "Does the lodge have a fax machine?" he asked. It did. "Can I use it to fax this to Pittsburgh?"

"Of course." Charlie showed him where the fax machine was and left him to his work.

Caputo returned shortly, Ron and Anthony were still in the office, talking to Charlie. All three looked up at him anxiously when he entered. "Well, at least that's done. I just hope someone recognizes and knows this guy."

"You mean you don't know who he is?" asked Ron.

Shaking his head, Caputo admitted that until now only he and the two women in Pittsburgh had recognized him. "It's scary, he's probably committed murders in at least three states and nobody has come forward with any information until just recently."

"How is that possible?"

"The only thing I know is that he's been careful. The victim in Ohio was the first to be identified as a homicide, the others were thought to be accidental. He moves around, changes his name, makes up a new past." Caputo picked up the new composite, "With his looks, he could warm up anybody."

229

"He is good looking," Ron said.

"That he is. I wonder what would make someone as attractive, and most likely intelligent, as him kill?" Charlie asked.

"Police in Ohio have a theory, but we won't know for sure until he's caught."

"What is their theory?" Ron asked absently.

"Well," Sergeant Caputo began, "According to their psychologist, this guy was probably sexually abused as a child…"

"So were many others. They didn't start killing people."

"I know. That was a question I had as well. What was it that make him start killing?"

"Were you able to come up with any answers?"

"We think so."

The small room became eerily silent as Caputo, staring into some unseen distance, filled in the missing pieces of the man whose killing they hoped to put an end to.

"It's not easy to explain," he started hesitantly, "But if the profile developed in Ohio is correct he's suffering from something called paranoid schizophrenia."

The others looked confused. "And that is?" asked Ron.

"Its a neurologial disorder, somewhat similar to that of a person who has multiple personalities."

"He's like Sybill, then?" inquired Anthony.

"No. Not really." Caputo got up and began pacing, all eyes following him as he continued completing the picture of the killer. "Sybill had many personalities, 17 in all, I think. Someone who suffers from paranoid schizophrenia doesn't develop other personas."

"What do you mean?" Ron asked as he sat up, intrigued by the unfolding of the layers of this man's psyche.

"If I'm correct in what I've read in the reports, this particular disorder is characterized by several distinct traits. The individual has a very disturbed thought patterns, they believe thoughts are literally implanted into their minds."

"Like they here voices?"

"Yes. Another characteristic is that they are usually loners, and if they do develop any interpersonal relationships they are generally abnormal."

"I'd say killing someone you're having a relationship with is pretty abnormal," interjected Anthony.

"There's one thing I'm confused about," said Ron, "What is it with older men? I mean, he appears to be having some sort of intimate relationship with them. What is it that makes him suddenly kill them?"

"Good question. From what I understand, people who have this disorder many times believe they are being persecuted, and judging from the supposed sexual abuse that seems to be the case here. He is most likely fighting two very powerful forces, his attraction to older men and his disturbed thoughts of persecution by older men."

"Why doesn't he just walk away if he feels threatened by these men?"

"I think that's when everything starts to change for him. He's put into a fight or flight situation. I'm sure there were times in the past where he would have chosen flight. But his thoughts have become so disturbed and the voices so pronounced that he can no longer choose that avenue, he must fight."

"Fighting is one thing. Killing, however, is a bit extreme, isn't it?"

"To us it is, but don't forget, he starts to see these men as a threat to his very existence, and they have to be eliminated. I guess you could say he's a lot like Norman Bates in Psycho."

"My God!" sighed Ron.

Sitting down again, Caputo looked around at the stunned, silent group. "Now you know about as much as we do."

Getting up, Ron said in a cold voice, "I hope they catch him soon. Is there anything else we can do, Sergeant?"

Folding his hands on the desk, Sergeant Caputo said, "Truthfully, yes, there is something I'd like to discuss with you two. We have an idea that might get this guy out in the open. Let me explain it to you then decide if you're able, and willing to help. It would involve both of you and there could be some risk."

Ron looked at Anthony then back to Sergeant Caputo, "What's your idea?"

He quickly filled them in and waited for a response. Both men nodded and Anthony answered for both of them, "Let's do it." Caputo thanked them both as he picked up the phone and began dialing. Ron and Anthony quietly left, knowing he had much to do.

Sergeant Caputo and his partner spent the day with Ron and Anthony, sledding, building snowmen with the other guests, and going for a long walk, taking pictures, anything to be highly visible. By the end on the day, all four men were exhausted. They got drinks, hot chocolate, and coffee, and sat in the lobby with Officers Landis and Collins. The only other people in the lobby were Gary and Tim.

Leslie had checked on Gary several times during the day, the wound looked good, no redness or swelling, and still no fever. Before she and Joan, her girlfriend, went for dinner, Gary asked if she was a doctor, since she was so knowledgeable. She laughed, "No. I'm an E.M.T. in Boston. Believe me, I've seen a lot worse than this. You're lucky, you'll be up and around in no time."

"Speaking of being up, when can I get up? Lying here is driving me nuts!"

Leslie studied him for a moment, "Maybe tomorrow, but only with help. You're healing well. I'd hate to see you open the wound. Remember, you have to heal on your own since there was no way to suture you up. Tim, is there any more peroxide or betadine here?"

"Sure, in the kitchen."

"I'd like you to wash the wound every few hours and change the bandages. Can you do that?"

"Of course, I'd be glad to."

Leslie and Joan left for dinner, asking Officers Landis and Collins to join them. They glanced over to Caputo, who nodded slightly, then left.

Ron and Anthony soon excused themselves as well. They thanked Sergeant Caputo, now know to them as Carmine and his partner, Sean Ryan, for a fun day and hoped that their plan would have the desired affect. After a while, Sean said he was going out on the porch for a smoke, Tim joined him. Standing in the cold, clear evening they struck up a conversation, talking about their careers, the weather and of course, the events of the past 24 hours.

"I hope you catch him. We'll all feel much better when he's behind bars."

Flipping his cigarette, Sean replied, "He'll be caught. I don't think he's gone anywhere, especially in this storm. He's probably right under our noses." He walked to the far edge of the porch, "How much property to this complex?"

"Oh, I'm not really sure. About 20 to 30 acres. Jonathan and Charlie are planning some major changes this year," he pointed across the road, "Including getting those cabins heated."

A stunned look flashed across Sean's face. "Cabins! What cabins?"

"There," Tim pointed, "Up behind those trees. You wouldn't even know they were there, would you? We tried to get the former owners to..." Tim suddenly found himself talking to no one as Sean was nowhere in sight and the door to the lodge slammed shut.

Sean spoke in animated whispers to Carmine, who immediately got up and rushed to the dining room door. He motioned for Collins and Landis, who politely excused themselves and left a confused Leslie and Joan sitting at the table.

"What's up? Did you spot him?" Collins asked as they hurried to the corner of the lobby. Sean joined them and in a huddled group Carmine relayed his information.

"Cabins, what cabins?" Landis asked.

"On the far side of Mt. Nebo Road, up behind that stand of evergreens. Get Charlie or Jonathan in here pronto!"

"Christ." Collins said, "I didn't even know they were there!"

"None of us did. Remember when we came in it was already dark and we were in the back of the snow plow. Sean and I were out most of the day, but down the mountainside, on the other side of the lodge."

Both Charlie and Jonathan arrived and Carmine turned his attention to them, "Why didn't you tell us about the cabins?" Stunned by the edge of his voice and embarrassed by their own neglect, neither man could respond. They simply looked at each other in shocked disbelief at their omission of this bit of important information.

"I'm sorry. That's not important now. What we need to know is how many there are, how many rooms in each, how many doors, windows. I'm positive he's in one of them, probably the first or last."

Charlie gave them the information. There were three cabins, one room and a small bathroom in each. The only door was the front one and there were windows on all four sides of each. They were closed up for the winter.

Thinking quickly, Caputo outlined a simple plan. He and Sean would approach the first and last cabin from the front, Collins and Landis from the rear, guns drawn. On his signal, he and Sean would kick in the doors. The noise, even if he wasn't in one of those two cabins, should be enough to scare him into the open. "He'll more than likely crash through a back window, so you two," he pointed to Collins and Landis, "Be ready. Any questions?"

"Yeah," Landis asked, "If we have to fire?"

"Hit him anywhere you can, but try to stop, not kill him. I want this bastard to stand trail. Let's get ready."

Dressed in black flack uniforms, communicators checked and attached at the shoulder, flashlights and guns ready, they headed out. Jonathan and Charlie stood nearby, anxious and scared. As he rechecked his gear, Caputo told them to keep everybody inside. "Tell them anything you want to, but do not let them leave the lodge."

"All right," they nervously agreed.

Scanning his team, Caputo gave the final order to move out.

Watching the team move out into the cold night, Charlie asked, "What do we do?" How are we going to keep everyone here in the lodge?"

"Let me think for a minute." Jonathan's eyes darted back and forth in his head as he considered possibilities. "Okay, first we check the dining room, if it's full, that means most of the guest are here and we can tell them to stay for a special event we've planned, due to the blizzard."

"A special event? Like what?"

Jonathan thought as he paced, picking his lower lip. He stopped short, "I've got it! We can tell them that we've decided to have a Commitment Ceremony here for Ron and Anthony. They'll go for that. Won't they?"

"How should I know? You're the one who thought of it. They weren't really going to have a Commitment Ceremony, were they?"

"They are now!"

"What do we do about the people who aren't here?"

Jonathan's face grew serious. "We have to check the other buildings. Anyone in Mt. Nebo House will be safe, that building is far enough down the mountain. We'll just tell them to stay put for a while. Make up something about downed power lines, or ice, anything. Rainbow House is a different story, that building is right next to the cabins. If there's gunfire..." They shared a worried glance. "Okay, you hit the dining room then get Ron and Anthony ready. Tell them it's our gift to them. I'll go over to Rainbow House and check it. I hope to God it's empty. Hurry!" Jonathan was gone before Charlie could respond. He took a deep breath and went directly into the kitchen, telling the staff the truth about the situation, then their plan. Fear and shock were evident on their faces. Without waiting for a verbal reaction, he went back into the dining room, turned off the music and asked for everyone's attention. When it got quiet, he made the fictitious announcement about Ron and Anthony's ceremony.

Most of the guests were pleased and excited. "So stay put, enjoy your meal, and we'll get the ceremony started shortly. Remember, this is a gift from us, and a surprise, so don't blow it, so to speak." The crowd laughed at his unintentional pun. Charlie was running on pure adrenalin, his body trembled and he was perspiring heavily. He knew his voice was shaky, but hoped no one noticed. He ran through the kitchen and out the rear door to the small house NuView occupied. Harold answered his insistent knocking.

Seeing the look on Charlie's face, he was instantly alarmed, "What's wrong? Get in here!" He pulled Charlie in and slammed the door. Breathing heavily, he asked where Ron and Anthony were.

"We're right here," Ron said. They were sitting a few feet from him, on the sofa. "Charlie, what the hell is wrong" You look terrified!"

Ray and Steve heard the commotion and came in.

"Look, all I can tell you is this," looking directly at Ron and Anthony, he continued, "You two are having a Commitment Ceremony here, tonight, in the dining room. Get dressed."

Anthony began to protest, "We're what? What ever gave you the idea that we even wanted a ceremony?"

Taking a deep breath, Charlie explained the recent events, "Now hurry!"

The alarmed men dressed quickly but had to wait for Harold. He emerged from the bedroom dressed in a floor length ivory evening gown, gloves, jewelry, and a fur wrap. The others stared at him in disbelief. "This isn't a show!" Ron exclaimed, holding back nervous laughter.

In a dead serious voice, Harold replied, adjusting his gloves, "This, my dears, is probably the most important performance we'll ever do. We're not only entertaining we may just save someone's life." That reality struck all of them hard. Picking up his beaded bag, Harold opened the door, "Let's go."

Jonathan returned and found Charlie in the kitchen, "Rainbow House is empty. Is everything set here?"

Charlie nodded, his entire body trembling and his skin pasty white. Jonathan held him close, stroking his matted hair, "Hey, its okay. We'll be all right. We lived in Manhattan for years, things like this happened there all the time, remember?"

"Yeah, but not right in front of us. Not in our own home! I've never been so scared in my whole life. Why are you so calm?"

Hugging him tighter, Jonathan softly answered, "I'm just as scared as you, as any of us. I don't know what happens to me, but something inside takes over during any kind of crises. Believe me, when this is all over, I'll be a basket case and you can comfort me."

"Come on," Jonathan said to Charlie, "Let's start the ceremony."

Pulling back, Charlie said, "Wait a minute, who is going to be conducting this so called ceremony?"

Everyone in the kitchen looked at everyone else, none of them had even thought of that. After several moments of absolute silence, a voice from the back of the room answered, "Oh, what the hell, I'll do it." It was Frank, one of the waiters.

"You!" Helen howled.

"Hey, it'll just be another form of drag, and I do look good in basic black."

"Do you think he call pull it off?" Charlie asked.

"Do we have any other choice?" Jonathan asked in response.

Harold pushed through the small, crowded kitchen, "Well, honey, let's get you ready. You're on in 15 minutes." He took over orchestrating the mock ceremony. He finished his instructions to Ron, Anthony, Charlie, and Jonathan just as Frank returned dressed in what could pass for cleric's robes, "I'm ready!"

Carmine and Sean quietly got into position, crouching low on the small porch of the first and last cabins. Collins and Landis signaled that they were ready. "On three," Carmine whispered into his mike. Both doors blew in simultaneously, wood splintering, dust and debris filling the cold air. Antone' reacted instantly and on pure instinct. As the door crashed to the floor and Carmine entered, gun drawn, flashlights sweeping arcs of dusty light through the single room cabin, he lunged head first out the back window, slamming into Officer Collins, knocking her into the drifted snow. Scrambling to his feet he kicked her viciously in the chest and face, breaking ribs, and her nose, before running into the woods and up the steep slope behind the cabins. He heard frantic voices and saw beams of flashlights dancing behind him.

His primal urge to survive took over. He plowed his way through the snow, up Mt. Nebo, clawing at the branches that reached out to snare him. He ducked to avoid these imaginary arms, at times stumbling, having to crawl on all fours, but he kept moving. He dared not look back, but his ears scanned the terrain like R.A.D.A.R. for any sound other than his own breathing and pounding heart. He heard nothing. Sweat seeped onto his eyelashes, crystallizing instantly.

In the dark forest, under a luminescent full moon, he saw a light ahead of him. Could one of his pursuers have gotten ahead of him? No, that wasn't possible. He wiped crystals from his eyelashes and tried to focus. It was a light, a light from a house, then another. This renewed his resolve and he plunged ahead energized by the new possibility of escape. By now, his jeans were soaked, and the soles of his boots gave him almost no traction in the deep, slippery snow.

He came to a clearing and took a chance on looking back. There in the distance he could still see the bouncing beams of two flashlights. They were closer than he thought they'd be. He started to run again, but stumbled and fell, slamming his right knee into a jagged rock hidden under the snow. He let out an angry scream, but got up and tried to run. The pain shot through his entire leg, and slowed his pace considerably.

Caputo and Ryan were now closing in on him fast. Once at the clearing, Caputo saw the colorful sweater bobbing on the other side, then he saw the lights of the houses in the newly constructed Sunrise Hills development. If they didn't get to him before he got to one of those houses... Caputo didn't let himself finish that thought, he quickened his pace instead. Plunging ahead, fueled by this new fear, he gained several yards. He saw 'Paul' stumble, then get up. "Now!" he told himself and fired. 'Paul went down, and Caputo thought it was over, but 'Paul' got up and, limping badly, pushed on to the backyard of the nearest house. Caputo fired again. This time 'Paul' went down and stayed there. Caputo remained in his crouched position for a moment, then holstered his weapon. He alerted Sean, who was soon at his side. Carmine was breathing heavily, more from the mental exhaustion than physical. Sean put his arm around his partner, "You okay?"

Still panting, Carmine slowly stood, "Yeah, I'm fine. Let's check on him."

They slowly approached the man they knew as Paul Zimza, Sean with his weapon still drawn. 'Paul' lie face down in the snow, motionless. Sean nudged the body with his toe, no response. Rolling him over, it was obvious that he was dead, there was a large exit wound above his right eye, Carmine's second shot. Sean looked up at Carmine, "Nice shot."

"I wasn't aiming for his head, but the way he was limping from the first bullet, my aim must have been off. Too bad, I really wanted to bring him in to stand trial."

Holstering his gun, Sean said, "Well, at least it's over. Come on, let's get him back down to the cabin."

Carmine shook his head, "Fuck him, let him lie here. The locals can get him."

They turned and walked back to the lodge.

Local police and ambulances were already there when they got back to the lodge, the lights of their vehicles ripping through the darkness. "Turn those damned things off!" Caputo screamed, "We know you're here!"

Collins was sitting up in an ambulance, being attended to by the paramedics. She was pretty banged up, but would be okay. Gary had been put into another ambulance and was already en route to a hospital, Tim with him.

Sean told 2 uniformed officers where the body was. They grabbed a black body bag from the trunk of their squad car and headed off. "Oh, his last victim is in the tool shed, behind the lodge." They got another bag.

Many of the guests were on the porch, silently watching the events. As Sean and Carmine mounted the stairs, they parted, then followed them in. Carmine collapsed on the sofa, thoroughly exhausted. People milled about, talking in hushed groups, some going for drinks. Sean removed his flack jacket, and helped Carmine off with his. Sitting next to him and taking his hand, he asked Carmine if he wanted a drink.

"Yeah, a double scotch!"

"I'll get it," Charlie replied.

Jonathan stared at the two police officers who had just killed 'Paul', surprised by their intimacy.

Carmine grinned, "What's the matter?"

"Huh? Oh, nothing. I mean, I just..." he was at a loss for words, but continued staring at the two officers sitting across from him, holding hands.

"Surprise!" laughed Sean.

Charlie returned with drinks for everybody. "What's going on? What did I miss?"

Taking a sip of his drink, Carmine told Charlie that Jonathan was surprised to find out that he and Sean were gay. "So are Landis and Collins." Charlie's chin dropped as he plopped onto the chair next to Jonathan.

Carmine explained the events that brought them here. "After the realization that they were dealing with a homicide, and the possible serial, or pattern killer, Chief Myers contacted Agent Atkinson, the F.B.I. agent friend of his. He, in turn got in touch with the state police, of which G.O.A.L. is a part. Our captain approached us and asked if we would volunteer if needed. Of course we said yes.

"I guess when those women in Pittsburgh told Myers that they recognized the man in the composite and said he was heading to the

Philadelphia area, he got in touch with Atkinson again."

"We got the call, and the rest, you know." Sean finished the story.

"I didn't even know there was a gay cop group." Charlie said. Looking at Jonathan, he asked if he did.

"No not at all. Thank God there is! I can't imagine straight cops in an environment like this."

"It would be a bit difficult for them," Sean agreed, "Oh, Carmine, could you imagine Swenson here?"

Carmine roared. "Swenson is a gorgeous blond, about 6'3", body to die for and as soft spoken and sweet as they come, but as straight as an arrow."

"Straighter!" Sean corrected.

"He'd be hit on so much here he'd lose it. Probably end up running all the way back to headquarters!" Both cops laughed hysterically.

"Oh!" started Carmine, "Do you remember the time..."

Without anybody realizing it, things were returning to normal. The lodge and its out buildings regained their peaceful continence, and Mt. Nebo was once again calm, and safe.

The next afternoon most of the guests checked out, eager to return home and resume their private lives again.

The new millennium had begun.

Gil Burgess

EPILOGUE

GARY AND TIM

Gary recovered from his wounds and returned to Trenton, to pack. By April, he and Tim were settled in their new home near Stroudsburg. Gary's book had been published, and he did dedicate it to Leslie. He was feverishly working on his next novel entitled BLIZZARD.

Tim was finishing his work on a degree in hotel and restaurant management hoping to open a bed and breakfast in the near future.

RON AND ANTHONY

Ron and Anthony stayed with NuView until suitable replacements were found. When that was done, they said their good-bye's and left to find a house in a warm climate. Ron never wanted to see snow again.

JONATHAN and his FATHER

A week after the incident, with room 6 cleaned, refurnished and repainted, Lambda Lodge was quiet. Stacy was at the front desk when an older gentleman entered and asked to see Jonathan. She went to get him.

The man's back was to him when Jonathan entered the lobby, "How can I help you?" he asked, then stood in amazement as the man turned and he recognized him, "Dad!"

Chief Myers had his son in his arms in seconds, holding him in a vice like grip. "When I heard, when I found out what happened! Oh, Jonathan, I was so afraid I'd lose you. I'm so sorry. Can you ever forgive me?"

Stacy and Charlie watched from the dining room doors, arms wrapped around each other, lips trembling as tears formed in their eyes.

"Ah, Dad!" was all Jonathan could say as he continued to be held by his father.

Eventually the embrace ended. Jonathan looked over and saw Charlie. "Come on, Dad, there's someone I'd like you to meet." He introduced Charlie who extended his hand. Chief Myers shook it then pulled Charlie into a warm embrace.

The three men went into the dining room for coffee, their conversation focusing on the events of last week. "Jonathan stayed so calm." Charlie told Chief Myers. "I was a wreck!"

"I'm not surprised," Chief Myers said confidently, "After all, he is my son."

MILLIE and ADELLE

Mille stood watching the morning news. She could not believe that nice young man was a murderer. She called Adelle, who had already seen the story in the morning paper. "I still can't believe it was him, but his room was empty, he never intended to return."

"Now I'm glad we made that call. At least we know we helped."

"Me too." Adelle hung up and continued reading the whole story of the others that were murdered by this "nice young man."

THE POLICE

Police Departments in Chicago, Dayton and Denver started to receive calls with bits of information. Together they tried to discover the true identity of the serial killer. The only names they kept coming up with, however, were in his aliases. No one seemed to know who he really was.

To this day his true identity remains a mystery.

ARIZONA

Sitting in her wheel chair in the day room at the Desert Nursing Home outside Phoenix, sipping tea, Gloria Albertson glanced up at the television set. The face on the screen looked familiar, too familiar. She put down the cup and wheeled herself closer to the screen. Staring at the drawing she gasped, it couldn't be. She stared harder, but the camera turned back to the reporter. She asked for a newspaper and when she got it, quickly scanned for the story. In shock, she read what had happened to those men. Her hands shaking badly, she looked back at the drawing again. As tears dropped on the newsprint, she touched the drawing, "I'm so sorry I didn't do anything to help."

ABOUT THE AUTHOR

G. Burgess started his writing career as a poet. His work in this field won him election as a Distinguished Poet in the International Society of Poets.

He moved to writing short stories, mainly for the entertainment of his 5th grade students. He continued writing on his own for a while, then decided to take writing classes offered by a local college. He studied writing under noted mystery author, Jane Waterhouse and with her encouragement went on to write his first book. At present he is studying screen writing with Ike Evans through the same college extension.

Born and raised in Highland Park, New Jersey he now lives in historic Freehold, New Jersey. He received his BS Degree from Monmouth University and his M.Ed. Degree from The College of New Jersey. He has been an elementary school teacher in Edison, New Jersey for the past 31 years. This is his first book.

Printed in Great Britain
by Amazon

17856671R00161